IN THE
MIDDLE
OF ALL THIS

ALSO BY FRED G. LEEBRON

Postmodern American Fiction:
A Norton Anthology (coeditor)

Out West

Creating Fiction: A Writer's Companion (coauthor)

Six Figures

FRED G. LEEBRON

IN THE
MIDDLE
OF ALL THIS

HARCOURT, INC.
New York   San Diego   London

Requests for permission to make copies of any part of the work
should be mailed to the following address: Permissions Department,
Harcourt, Inc., 6277 Sea Harbor Drive, Orlando, Florida 32887-6777.

www.HarcourtBooks.com

*This is a work of fiction. All the names, characters, places, organizations,
and events portrayed in this book are either products of the author's
imagination or are used fictitiously for verisimilitude. Any other resemblance
to actual people, organizations, or events is unintended.*

Library of Congress Cataloging-in-Publication Data

Leebron, Fred.
In the middle of all this/Fred G. Leebron.—1st ed.
p.   cm.
ISBN 0-15-100834-5
1. Brothers and sisters—Fiction.   2. Cancer—Patients—Fiction.
3. London (England)—Fiction.   4. College teachers—Fiction.
5. Married People—Fiction.   6. Pennsylvania—Fiction.   I. Title.
PS3562.E3666 I6   2002
813'.54—dc21
2001005955

Text set in Minister Light
Display set in Gagamond
Designed by Cathy Riggs

Printed in the United States of America
First edition
A C E G I K J H F D B

For Kathryn, Cade, and Jacob
and
Kathryn Smyth

ACKNOWLEDGMENTS

Many, many thanks to Amanda Urban and Jen Charat for their wonderful guidance and complete support and encouragement. I'm also grateful to Steve Rinehart, J. D. Dolan, Peter Ho Davies, Andrew Levy, André Bernard, and the incomparable Don Lee for their diligence, wisdom, and generosity. Thanks as well to Lynne Raughley, Barry Wolfman, Janet Rollings, Elizabeth Lambert, Christopher Fee, and Ian Clarke for their help and tolerance.

For support during the writing of this book, thanks to the Pennsylvania Council on the Arts and Gettysburg College.

I am most grateful to Kathryn Rhett, for her editorial expertise, patience, and kindness.

What if I did not mention death to get started
Or how love fails in our well-meaning hands

—ROBERT HASS, "THIN AIR"

IN THE BONE

The ride from the SuperGiant cut through one of the most blood-soaked stretches of land in the country's history, and in the backseat Martin Kreutzel's seven-year-old daughter and two-year-old son pointed and wondered at the long rows of obelisks, vaults, and statues. THEY DIED LIKE MEN, a billboard said. EVEN THE TWELVE-YEAR-OLDS. On the battlefield tourists paced the steps they imagined others had taken, or followed the pull of frantic metal detectors. "How many there?" Sarah asked as they passed a wide gray slab dedicated to Alabama's volunteers. "How many there?" Martin warily eyed the totals of killed, wounded, and missing. "One hundred and seventy," she said. Sarah was a great reader. "That's killed," she told Max. "Daddy, you're driving too fast for me to catch it all."

"Okay, okay." He made himself slow down despite the ice cream and milk in the trunk, a line of cars snarling ahead anyway, the air-conditioning in his old Honda vibrating and waning. Red clapboard barn houses hid in the swells of the valley, and on a hillock a dozen black-and-white milk cows drowsily grazed. An oncoming car from Tennessee—Martin couldn't resist noting all the license plates—inexplicably flashed its lights at him, and the driver pointed. Then a station wagon from Texas honked at him—Martin flinched, thinking it was yet another redneck who wanted directions to where Great Grandpappy had taken his last breath—and the guy rolled down his window.

"You got a flat," the Texan called.

Martin shrugged. He couldn't feel a thing. But he pulled over, alongside a raised sundial honoring the men of South Carolina. "Stay put," he told the kids. He got out: the driver's side was clear. He walked around back. No problem there. But the right front tire sagged as if shot.

"What the hell?" he said. He had had the tires changed last year, and he couldn't see a nail or a long shard of glass or a gaping hole or the leftover shred of a blowout. The tire was just flat. He peeked through the sunshade at the children. They were quiet.

Martin clicked open the hatchback and began to pull out all the grocery bags.

"I have to change a tire," he said. "It'll only take a minute."

"Can't we get out?" Sarah asked. "We're burning hot in here."

"Yeah," Max said.

There wasn't a useful tree within a hundred yards. But if he could make it to Wyatt's Charge, there was a shaded pullover. He dumped the groceries back in and slammed the hatchback.

"One second," he told them.

He waited for a space between cars and then limped the Honda onward. At least it was a fine day. At least they weren't more than a mile from home. At least he had done this before. At the pullover he rushed the $140 of wilting groceries from the car and dug out the jack and the donut. Miraculously the children remained still. His hands on the jack trembled mildly. Most people in the Anthropology Department had the shakes, but they were older. He told himself he was too young for the shakes and started cranking.

He and Lauren and the kids had moved here only a year ago, but it had been a year of inch after inch of rainwater in the basement of their new home, a year of a witch in their department gunning for them in the usual insidious ways, a year when his dad suffered through prostate cancer and his sister in London learned that she had forty tumors on her spine. *Forty tumors on her spine,* his new colleagues said. *How could that be?* And he'd had to explain the tiny calcifications in her breasts that had gone unremarked, the months of general back pain and visits to physical therapists and chiropractors and charlatans, and finally the bone scan that had lit her up. And then it had become a year when he woke every morning feeling oppressed and paranoid only to discover that his presentiments were justified. It had become a year that he and Lauren bandied about words like *grace* and *mercy*—words he had never used—and debated just what the fuck they meant. It had been a year of death, he decided—this first year they had lived here—a lot of imminent death, and a lot of rain that had nothing to do with growth and everything to do with being buried.

"All right," he muttered, "all right."

When he was finished—not with this particular thought, he wasn't finished with that—the donut, compared to the adult-sized chassis, looked like something from a toy, but the whole enterprise had taken only fifteen minutes, and the groceries when he resituated them appeared to cling to a last level of freshness. The day was still blue and bold, autumnal save for the slight heat. His head was in a mild sweat. He'd get the kids home, set them in front of the TV for their one show, shove the groceries into the fridge, and have almost an hour to make himself concentrate and complete the last of the syllabi for his three courses. Then he'd treat himself to a Bloody Mary or a beer.

"Here we go," he said.

It was odd how silent they were. Maybe it was on account of all the men who had died here, maybe it was because of the heat, maybe it was the car—or the ice cream—that worried them.

"Cheer up," he told them, "we're right on schedule."

"Okay," Max said. But Sarah kept her eyes shut as if she were trying to sleep. Had he said something mean? He couldn't remember.

At Union Street, Martin stopped as a double-decker tour bus groaned past, the folks grouped on the open top, listening to a guide with a megaphone. *Carnage* and *slaughter* were the only words he caught.

"Double-decker!" Max said.

When Martin started the car across Union, it rolled forward several feet and then seemed to fall on its face, as if he'd lost a tire, and it ground to a halt in the middle of the intersection. In the distance vehicles approached.

"Daddy!" Sarah shouted. *"Daddy!"*

He crushed the accelerator, grating the car across as its metal scraped against asphalt and its rear fishtailed. He pulled over onto the battlefield.

Sarah's arm was flung over her eyes and she was silently crying.

"What happened?" Max said, pulling against the straps of his car seat. "What happened?"

"That wasn't so bad," Martin said, trying to smile. "Was it?"

"We almost got hit," Sarah mourned.

"All right now. Take it easy."

Again he tore out for a look. Under the heavy axle the donut seemed as thin as a crepe.

"Fuck," he said. "Fuck!"

Now what?

In the Honda the children squirmed. Out-of-state cars sailed up and down Union. The line of monuments curved east and west around the town. At least he wasn't out on the interstate. This wasn't in the middle of nowhere.

He got in and made the car drag itself over as far as it could. He got out and stared at it. Unbelievable, just fucking unbelievable. Of all the—goddamn it. Goddamn. Man. He drew in as much air as he could, held it, let it out, drew air in again. Again. Okay. Again. He went around and softly pulled Max from his car seat, carried him back to Sarah's side, and let her out.

"Daddy, I'm hot," she said.

"I know. I know." He nudged Max. "Can you walk?"

Max shook his head. His hair fell down between his eyes and his cheek bulged, and he sank into a patch of his own drool on Martin's shoulder. "Tired," he said.

"Carry *me*," Sarah said.

He gave her his hand. "You know I can't."

He said his good-bye to the groceries, and they labored down the cannon-lined road around Cemetery Hill, the sun on their necks, the boy snoring. The late summer air was full of the green smell of cut grass and crisped cornstalks and bundled straw, and soon Martin felt his breathing slow, his pulse dip almost to normal. There was so much worse, he told himself, than two flat tires and a lost week of groceries. So much worse that it was all practically unspeakable. He kept hold of Sarah's hand.

"Please, Daddy," she said, but she seemed resigned.

Later they walked past the railed Alms House Cemetery, a white stone planted at the heart of each abbreviated plot, and it suddenly struck him that there had been dead under the fields before they fought the great battle of the Civil War, and then there were thousands and thousands more dead when they finished, and he marveled at the enormous number of dead there must be in the world. Maybe there was some solace in that.

———

"Marty?"

Perhaps he was just imagining it. He kept walking, Max's warm face against his, Sarah's mushy hand still holding on.

"Marty!"

They turned. The co-chair of Anthropology had pulled alongside in his car. Martin nodded at the boy to indicate he was asleep and at the girl to show she was burning hot.

"Very sweet," Ruben said, stopping the car. "Look, you got a minute?"

"I really should—"

"My wife's just been fired." Ruben threw up his hands and dragged himself from the car. His face was dark and unshaven, his hair was in his eyes, and his lips were trembling.

Martin stopped.

"Daddy," Sarah murmured.

"Julia goes into work today," Ruben said, his voice shrill, "at eight A.M., an hour ahead of everybody, just as usual, and she can't open the door. She tries one key, then another, then a third. She thinks she's losing her mind." He stopped himself, breathing hard, and stared past the wriggling boy at Martin. "Does any of this make any sense to you?"

"No way," Martin said, although it sounded a little like what had happened to his father years ago, when he came home early from work wearing a papier-mâché life preserver that said SS Titanic.

"Exactly. So she tries all the keys again. She's practically a damn partner in the place, and she can't even get into her own fucking office. At a pay phone she calls the CEO. And the CEO says, 'We've changed all the locks. Yesterday was your last day.'"

"Can they do that?" Martin asked as Max whimpered and Sarah tugged at him. "I mean, wasn't there notice or a warning?"

"Nothing. The damn CEO was sleeping with the damn director of human resources, and they've engineered this thing from a long way off. Total subterfuge. Julia's been there twenty-two years, twenty-two fucking years, built the business from the ground up. Worked double the hours of anybody else. And they've gone and fired her." He snapped his fingers. "Just like that."

"Jesus," Martin said.

"Daddy, please," Sarah muttered.

"I'm on my way to our lawyer. What a numb nut that guy is. 'That's just the way it is,' he tells me on the phone." He pushed back the hair from his eyes. "So who's your lawyer?"

"Same as David Lazlo's," Martin said. "He did great at our closing, and I think he's going to do our will. But really I've got to—"

"What's a boy like you need a will for?" Ruben said. "But he's good, right? Only the best for David. I came in with that jerk, and now he's better off than I am."

"He's a force of nature," Martin said, beginning to move off again with the kids.

Ruben shook his head, climbing back in the car. "Or something," he said. "Sorry I kept you guys." He started the car and leaned across to the open window. "This all kind of reminds me of your sister. Not that it's really like it, you know, but just how you can get the crap permanently whacked out of you any minute of the week. I hope your sister's all right. What are you doing hauling around your kids this far out anyway?"

"Two flat tires," Martin said.

Ruben looked away and then looked back at Martin. "You see. That's exactly what I mean. You need a ride?"

The children were sweating and the sun was branding the back of his neck, and he could just imagine their conversation if he climbed into the car.

"Absolutely," he said.

By the time they were dropped at home, Max had again fallen asleep, and Martin laid him on the sofa and with quivering hands untied and took off his shoes while Sarah commandeered the television. In the kitchen he called Triple A and arranged a tow job, then he hurriedly dialed his sister's number in London. The double pulse began to ring in his ear.

"Hello?" his sister said.

"Hey," he said. "It's me. Is this a bad time?"

"Nope. I'm just sitting here waiting for Richard to get back from a course."

"Oh, right." He hadn't wanted to sound disapproving. He had wanted to tell her something of the battlefield and the flat tires, but as soon as he heard her voice he knew it was the wrong story.

"Now, now. It's good for him. It's good for us. Here, check this out. This is something he brought home last night."

"Okay," Martin said reluctantly. "Go ahead."

"Say you're interviewing for a job, and you get the job, and they're excited and you're excited and you agree to terms, and then a few days later the offer letter comes, and there's an extra zero on the salary—it's ten times what it's supposed to be. What do you think?"

"What do I think?" Martin laughed.

"Let me finish. Do you think: A) They've made a mistake and I should call them; B) They've made a mistake but I'll lie low and see if somehow that mistake can continue to happen; or C) They've changed their mind and decided that this is really what I'm worth."

"Ten times the salary? *What I'm worth?* Be serious."

"But don't you see?" She caught her breath. "That's exactly it. What if you could believe in C? What if you could start looking at yourself and the way you relate to the world in terms of C? What then? That's what the Epiphany courses are really all about."

"Interesting," Martin said. Though there was only one word he could associate with C, and he couldn't utter that.

"Don't dismiss it. Don't you dare dismiss it—"

"I'm not."

"I know, I know. Just keep an open mind for me, okay?"

"Are you in a lot of pain?" Martin asked gently.

"Can't you hear it?" She sighed. "Mom's on me again about chemo, and I give her back whatever she gives me, so really our conversations these days are all poison."

"I wish you guys would—"

"It's really stressful," Elizabeth said. "I don't need the stress. Then Martha called, and I had to take her on, too. You're the only one who doesn't give me grief."

"I do."

"Well, it's the good grief, then. Or I don't notice it. Anyway, Richard's only gone till nine. When you coming over again?"

He looked at the clock. He really should get to work. "I just got back last week," he said.

"But that was without the wife and kids. I want you all. Aren't I terrible?"

"*No,*" he said.

"Sounds like you have to run."

"I guess I do."

"Thanks for the call. And kiss those kids of yours from me. And don't forget to send pictures. Or a video of them. I'd love a video."

"I will, I will."

"Bye," she said. "I've got to run, too."

"Bye."

He hung up the phone and shut his eyes. Sometimes he thought he was getting used to it, and sometimes he thought he had exhausted whatever he could feel about it, and sometimes he felt continuously rattled. He'd just been there, for chrissakes, and she was already asking him to bring the whole clan. An angry squeak jumped from somewhere in the house, and he looked at the front door before realizing it wasn't that.

"Up!" Max was screeching from the living room. "Up! *Get me!*"

Over dinner, which she had shopped hours for on too many different high streets, she began to notice an ache beyond the ache that she had recognized before, in the flank, in the pelvis. She rustled against it in the chair. Still there. Goddamn.

"What is it?" Richard said.

"Nothing," she lied. "Isn't this tofu excellent?"

"Oh, sure." But he stared at her. "Something new?"

"Maybe."

He pushed out from the table and stood behind her, touched thumbs to her shoulders, the circle of her neck. "Do you want to lie down?"

"A walk, I think."

They tied on their shoes and stepped into the empty street, the sun fallen, the dark cold. She headed them toward the park.

"I don't know that I want to walk very far," he said quietly, pushing his glasses up his nose and then taking her hand.

"I know." He had his evening meditation still. They walked and she winced, and by the end of the block she was wincing with every step.

"This is kind of sudden," she said.

"Maybe it will go away."

"It's sort of under the old one."

"Right."

"I can't even visualize the old one."

"Maybe it's nothing."

"Maybe."

"I hate that word," he said.

They walked along the fringe of the park under the lamplight, hearing a jangle of dog collar, the landing of a stick in the tall grass. *Oscar,* someone called. *Oscar.* The dog retreated into the deep dark. "Good evening," a man said from inside a falafel and ice-cream truck with an illuminated giant clown's face on top. "Something sweet for you this evening?" Elizabeth wanted to love their little neighborhood, the blunt, tightly packed houses; the barren black park; the high street with its dumpy, quirky, patched-up stores; the red letter boxes with their beret-like tops; the barred tube stop. A couple of years—not her favorite segment of time to think in—and maybe this could be like an outlying Hampstead. Martin kept telling her how much he liked it, but Martin was a nice liar. Martha, when she visited, scrubbed the floors and toilets, and then, because she had no idea what else to do for her, insisted on taking Elizabeth out for tea.

"What are you thinking about?" Richard nudged her. She turned them around. "My brother and sister."

"Those kids," Richard joked.

There was so little kidlike about them. Martha at forty-four had six squawking children and Martin drank so much that his personality was beginning to change. They hadn't played sports like she had, although Martin had tried; he'd just never been good. She used to wrestle him on the kitchen linoleum, and even when he finally got bigger he couldn't beat her. Martha had the back room, over the garage. Her bathroom smelled of Avon.

Elizabeth was the athlete, she was the health nut, she was the exerciser. Stop it, she muttered. Stop it.

They were nearing home. Richard gave up her hand so he could unlock the door. She punched in the code on the burglar alarm. He tiptoed up to the meditation room. The house, with all its leather and tile and marble and chrome, its recessed pin lighting against the London gray and cold, and its feng shui fabrics, ticked on.

In the kitchen—forty thousand pounds to renovate— she pulled out the day's third bag of vits and popped them three or four at a time—some stone colored, some orange-translucent, some capsules, some tablets, some round, one nearly square—until she'd done all fifty. Her blood work, Sparks said, was extraordinary. It's just that the spots didn't go away. One hundred and fifty pills a day and hormones and tinctures and herbs and teas, and still she had all those tumors. Why couldn't she just blast them out of her system? "A real accomplishment," Martin had tried to exult on the phone after yesterday's results. "If I could have prayed for anything nine months ago," Richard reminded her last night, "it would be for it to be the same." It was. She wasn't.

Everybody had to die. If she could have twenty more years, then it would be okay. Maybe even ten. She was eleven months past diagnosis.

Get out of your head, she thought. Just get out of your head. Get out now.

At least there was God. At least God was everywhere. At least when you opened your eyes every morning, there was the burnished dresser and the mango-colored window dressing and Richard pressing his glasses on and peering at you in that cryptic, warm way of his, as if to say, I know you, don't I, and I love you—yes, that's right. He could go into that narrow room with the two-thousand-quid Turkish carpet and the incense and the picture of Muyamaya, and he could will himself into an absolute clarity and purity. He'd said, when they'd first met, *You mean, you don't mind?* Of course not, she'd said. And from there on she'd joined his yoga group, traveling to retreats in California and in upstate New York and—when they moved to London—in Bridgetown. So much stillness you knew yourself. A different way to be inside your head. Not this American panic.

She listened for him. It had been only ten minutes. Sometimes she grew so impatient to have him back that she was tempted to set the microwave timer, but she couldn't bear to watch the time tick down anymore. And if she couldn't freeze it, then she'd expand it, she'd take the moment between each heartbeat and get inside of it and swell its engorged walls and make it tell her and show her everything she needed to know and see, and make it let her touch everything she needed to feel—to know it, to occupy it, to make it yours. Never to let it go because then it couldn't let you go. All this—as Martin would say—New Age shit, but without sounding terrible. Like he said all this work shit or all this love shit or all this family shit or all this medical shit.

She lay on the sofa under the new pain, feeling the terror, laid out under nothing. Passing. Passed. The pain was a tear along the brittle handle of her pelvis. The pain was a crack in the plate. If only the pain was all in her head. The way the bone scan would expose it. *Elizabeth,* Sparks would say, *Elizabeth, we're sorry but it's spread to the pelvis.* Sometimes she wished she'd never known, sometimes she wished she could always know, have scans once a day to help her track it, let her see that what she did was working. She needed to believe that she could know by the way she did what she was doing, but it was hard. It was hard not to feel it spreading, moving on to parts she hadn't even needed to be aware that she had, devouring her as it made room for itself. Why couldn't she believe?

"Sweetie?"

It was Richard, his face red, standing in the doorway.

"What?"

"What is it? You called," he stammered. "You called out."

"I did?" Now she was blushing, feeling inside to see if there was an answer.

"Oh yes." He stared at her. "You okay?"

"Sure," she said. "Sure."

He stood over her. "You're practically out of breath."

"Well." So it still hurt. Not a big deal. Just a little pain. Oh sure.

He sat beside her on the sofa. "You know the door's thick up there. I guess you must have screamed. Been screaming. Whatever."

"Okay," she said. "I mean," and she heard herself panting, "I'm okay."

"Do you want anything?"

"No," she said fiercely.

He touched the neckline of her blouse, held her hand. "You're soaked anyway. Maybe a bath with some salts."

"Yeah." You could lose what little hold you had on yourself so easily; its strength was less than tissue or thread. It was nothing. "Okay. I could do that."

"You want some help?"

"No." She swallowed to make sure she could say all the words. "You go finish. I'll be fine."

He stood, waiting.

"Go on," she said.

He looked at her sheepishly. "All right, then."

She shut her eyes to the sound of him padding up the stairs, clicking the thick door shut in the tiny room. He'd face the near wall, the one with the photograph, bend to his knees, descend to the carpet, glance once at the picture, bow his head, and rebegin. It's good that you already meditate, Sparks had told her. It will help. But that was after she'd said that nothing could cure her. It would help in the not helping. Sometimes she'd get on the tube and she'd look at all those people, the artsy university students and the schlubby civil servants and the buttoned-up corporate aggressors (one of whom she used to be) and think, we're all going to die. What did it matter? All of us. Soon. Sooner than probably anybody admits. In a transfer of records between one clinic and another, Sparks's notes fell into her hands. *Elizabeth makes it quite clear she doesn't want to talk about prognosis.* She'd shrieked when she read that. That was not it at all. She'd heard the prognosis once, and now and forever after she'd have to get past it and not rely on it, because then it was down to choosing which shoes to be buried in, how much money to parcel off for her nieces' and nephews' college. *You need to get your affairs in order.* If only you could keep it all in chaos, then maybe you weren't allowed to die. Once Richard had come home unexpectedly and caught her wallowing in the pages of her will, and he'd quickly, forcefully, silently shook his head, as if to say, Don't give up. You can't give up.

"We can do hormones," Sparks had told her the very first meeting, ticking off each item with her long, sleek fingers. "We can do drugs. We can take alternative measures. But at the end of the day"—she shook her head—"there's not much we can really do."

"Well, all that is something," Elizabeth had said.

"Yes, it's something," Sparks forced herself to agree.

"I am positive," Elizabeth said.

"Good." Sparks nodded. "That's good."

The student in Lauren's office wanted to register for a course that was long filled. Lauren dutifully tapped out an e-mail on his behalf, sent it, and sat staring at the screen, waiting to see if the return would be instant. The end-of-registration add/drop window slowly closed itself over the cables and in the corridors. They had twenty minutes left.

"I really need to get into this course," the advisee said, his face red and puffed. "It's why I came here."

It was David Lazlo's multimedia freshman seminar on the Civil War. Slide shows, films, radio plays, transcripts, diaries. It had been filled since June. It was forever filled.

"How much longer?" he whined. "My parents are waiting for me in my room."

Lauren swiveled toward him as he sat beside her. His parents were still here, but all parents had been dismissed at the end of the convocation two days before. "Look, Tristan," she said, recognizing the panic in his eyes. "You're not going to get in. There's a wait list twenty students long, and I think you need to move on with this."

"I *want* a freshman seminar," Tristan said, his face crumbling. "I *need* a freshman seminar."

She touched his elbow lightly. "It's not going to happen."

"Couldn't you call him?"

Though she considered Lazlo an ally of the junior faculty, he was the chair of the History Department and could be a bit regal. She picked up the phone and dialed.

"Professor Lazlo's office."

"Hi, Mary, it's Lauren. I've got a student here who really needs to get into David's freshman seminar."

"Lauren." Mary sighed. "I'm so sorry."

Lauren swiveled away from Tristan and dropped her voice. "His parents are still here."

"Sounds like he's one foot out the door already," Mary concurred. "I'll put you through."

Lauren glanced briefly at Tristan. His eyes were glistening. If he didn't get a fifth course, then she was really going to lose him. What would the dean of retention say?

"Is that Lauren?" David said thickly into the phone. "Lauren, my good friend. So good of you to call. I never hear from you often enough."

"Hey, David." He always laid on the irony. At least he was married to a genuine person; she had no idea how Cindy lived with him. "I've got a student here."

"A student? Imagine!"

"Yes, yes. And he'd love to be in your freshman seminar."

"Hah! Even the provost's daughter can't get into that course. Tell him to take the year off and try again."

"David?"

"Lauren, my child, if I give in to you, then all my other acolytes will—"

"Thanks a lot, David." She hung up.

"Tristan," she said, almost gaily.

He just looked at her.

Cognitive dissonance, she thought. Cognitive dissonance. "That Civil War stuff," she said, "is old history. It's recycled news. It's past yesterday. Is that what you want to devote your misery to?" She realized she'd been sitting inside too long, and on such a nice day. "Let's talk about something living, something breathing, something *right now*. Something that still matters. Biology. Management. Spanish. Whaddya say?"

"You're funny," Tristan sniffled. "But I want that course, I came here for that course, and if I'm not going to get that course"—he rose from his chair and smiled at her, smiled as if he'd known this was coming from the moment he signed his enrollment letter in the spring— "then I'm probably out of here."

Probably. That was something to latch on to.

"Film and the Vietnam War?" she tried, even though she knew it was full.

22

"Uh-uh." He shook his head. He pouted just like Max. She could have hugged him.

"Absolutely uh-uh?"

"Thanks for seeing me, Professor Kelly." He shook her hand, just like an adult.

"Don't forget our last orientation dinner tonight," she said gamely.

He smiled and shook his head again. Now he was an adult. Now he had made up his mind.

As he left, she called, "Tell your parents I said hello."

She sagged back in her chair, eyeing the door. Thirteen minutes to go. Maybe no one else was coming. Maybe she was done. It was hard to believe classes would begin tomorrow. It was hard to believe that in front of her stretched the whole appalling semester, the syllabi to distribute, the lectures to deliver, the discussions to pry from her students, the papers to assign and collect and grade and return, the department and committee meetings to attend, her own work to write, the trips to London to squeeze in. What little time—was it really only months now?—she and Martin had been told they had left with Elizabeth draining from them. The students indifferent, besieged, hostile, often medicated. Paxil or Prozac or Ritalin, she couldn't keep track. At a dinner party she'd once cornered a colleague from Residential Affairs and demanded to know how many students were on a prescription, their personalities sandblasted into blandness. "A lot," the colleague said, studying the label of his beer bottle. "But in percentages?" Lauren insisted. He shrugged. "Thirty?" Lauren guessed. The colleague began peeling back the label. "Forty?" The label curled slowly from the bottle. "Fifty?" He gave a slight but definitive nod and crumpled the label in his hand. Maybe it was better that Tristan left.

"Professor Kelly?" A student stood in the door. "Lauren?"

She squinted. She knew she needed glasses, but the ophthalmologist insisted she just needed to squint. She wondered if there was any more migraine medication in her briefcase.

"Come in," she said. "Sit down."

It was Jane Doyle, a sophomore, a departmental major, and Martin's advisee. She wore black lingerie and too-tight jeans.

"I'm dressing like my roommate," she explained.

"Oh." Lauren nodded.

"I was wondering if you'd talk to me about transferring."

"Transferring?" Lauren tapped the pen against her cheek.

Jane stared at her, rubbed her hands against each other. "It's really kind of awful here, you know."

Out Lauren's window the late summer sun was slowly tingeing the tall sugar maples rising from the quad. Where to begin, where to begin. It was only registration, for god's sake. She knew it was awful, but depending on your reasons any place could be awful. "How so?" she asked.

Jane gave a mock dramatic sigh. *"You know."*

She smiled wanly. "Tell me about it."

"The whole wretched J. Crew–Gap undergraduate culture, *of course*. The lazy, platitudinous professors. The shrinks over in Psychiatric Services who keep wanting to put me on medication. And, good god, there are just so many dead people here."

"I'm not even going to ask you what that's supposed to mean." Lauren pulled a folder from her desk drawer. "What about a year abroad?"

Jane glared at her. "I don't want to go to *England*. I don't want to go to *Germany*. I want to go to someplace anthropological, for god's sake." She took a breath. "I know, I know, humanity is everywhere." She was mimicking Martin's line, and they both smirked. "But sometimes it's more human other places."

"The Gap," Lauren pointed out, "is everywhere."

Now Jane looked out the window. "I probably couldn't get the same amount of aid anywhere else anyway."

"How do you know that?"

The student sneered. "So you *want* me to leave?"

They laughed. Martin and Lauren had coddled her all last year. But if she wanted to transfer, they had to help. Jane thumbed the strap of her top. Her pale face reddened.

"I am so bored, and I just got back," she said sadly.

"Everybody's on the brink." Lauren kept her voice smooth, touched the girl's wrist. "Sometimes the beginning can make you feel like that. That it's really a kind of cliff." She could strangle herself for this psychobabble. Atop the building the bell clock tolled; tiny reverberations rumbled from the floor. "We'll help you get a list together," she promised. "We'll help."

Jane rose, her face—Lauren saw with relief—composed. "I know," she said. "I guess you'd better be going. Tell Martin I'm still here."

"I will."

She strode from the room, her back stiffening in the inordinately revealing attire.

Since the Kappa Theta infanticide last year, Lauren felt that she ought to call Psychiatric Services at any hint of crisis, but, good grief, then they'd parachute in with all their medications and another personality would be dosed into remission. Sometimes all Lauren could see was that face, and sometimes she couldn't summon it at all, couldn't hear the voice. And she'd feel a panic and confusion rise within her. Was Cara short, was her voice bubbly? No one had even known she was pregnant. All those classes she sat through without uttering a word, all those empty smiles, all those careless nods of recognition and understanding, then that one Friday of chatterboxing, when she talked and talked in class, and afterward Lauren had said quietly, "Cara, are you all right." "Oh, sure," she'd said, "I'm great." Saturday night she'd dumped her newborn into a trash can at the Yankee Motel. I'm great. It wasn't, I'm not well. It wasn't, *Help me*. It was, I'm great. Great. She was great. She was serving three to five. Four weeks into their first semester, their house still in boxes, Max breast-feeding, Sarah a first grader, Elizabeth undiagnosed (a bad back, the doctors in London were thinking), the trees just turning. The student was a cheerful girl, she had a family, she doodled in class, she wrote gossipy columns for the newspaper, she had a roommate, she belonged to a sorority. She killed her own baby. Almost no one knew what to make of it. The president, a Canadian who insisted he was from Boston, had declared the matter private. The provost had counseled to keep in close contact with the students, to have a sense of them, to watch for danger signs. Campus Security had asked after anything unusual, and Lauren had confessed how Cara had talked and talked in class that day and that she had been wearing mirrored sunglasses until she'd been asked to take them off. Did they tape-record that conversation? Martin wanted to know, not in a paranoid way, just out of curiosity, just for the sake of speculation. She couldn't remember. The baby's death the newspapers called involuntary manslaughter, a turn of language that at first glance could make it sound as if the student had allowed her child to choke on a piece of food.

Lauren poked the necessary folders into her briefcase, locked shut the door, and stepped down the worn stairs to the lobby. In the empty quad the grass was deep green and newly mown, the trees stout and densely grooved. Along a distant asphalt path, the provost marched to his blue BMW. Atop the white administration building slumped an American flag.

She didn't have to feel deflated. A year was a long time, and they had gotten through it, and now it was a new year. New students—at least some. Now Sarah was in second grade, and Max was in day care two days a week. Now they continued in a steady, if vulnerable way. Martin was always flying off to be with Elizabeth, and at

Lincoln College there were always students falling off the edge. There was always *something*. That was what approaching forty was all about. The first mammogram, the first colonoscopy, the first biopsy.

She sped into the walk home. It was really just about getting blood to the brain and keeping it there, and then you never felt sucked under. You only felt speed. You could only keep moving. Otherwise, you'd drop. She blew by the houses on West Main, New England clapboard or redbrick, porticoes or screened porches, many windowed, two-toned painted shutters, dimensionally shingled roofs, gutters with custom guards, maple-fenced backyards. From the corner she could see to East Main where it met Fourth, could see that Martin had switched on the lamp over the front door in the fading daylight. Inside he'd be setting pots on the stove, rinsing vegetables, slicing skin from chicken or fish.

The wrong end of Main Street, everyone called it. The houses less stylish and kept up, the elementary school squatting opposite and beyond it the dulled shopping center, half ruined by a flood two summers past. *Don't worry,* the realtor had told them, *it was a once in a lifetime type of event.*

FALL

So, did you empty yourself out good for me?" Dr. Dowler smiled as he glanced briefly from the monitor.

Martin nodded, still dazed from all the laxatives. "Real good," he said.

"I'll have the nurse start the IV, and when the anesthesia kicks in, we'll proceed. Okay?"

"Okay."

The doctor stepped from the tight blue room.

"Just have to check on a few things," the nurse said. She examined the equipment, then turned to the gurney, where he lay on his side. She was about his age, maybe younger, with a wide, sunny face and a roll of fat around her waist. "We don't get many young guys in for this kind of thing," she said. "Something specifically you worried about, or family history?"

"Family history," he said.

"Let's hope you check out clear." She came around to face him and gently tugged at the neck of his gown and looked down the front of his chest to the rest of him and then let his gown fall back against him. She smiled. "Everything looks okay," she said.

Was she *checking him out*? A grin slopped over his numb face. She hummed to herself as she watched him and watched the IV and watched the monitor.

Soon—or was it later—Dowler came in. "How you feeling, Martin?"

"Good," Martin said.

"The monitor's right there, if you want to watch."

"In full color," Martin said.

"Yup."

Martin tried to stay awake for it, but his head was light, and his eyes heavy, and inside he was empty from the forced evacuation and the starvation diet, and he was drifting, falling. People had told him that it hurt so much you couldn't possibly sleep through it, but here he was, relaxed, all checked out, checking out. It wasn't so bad. It was nothing. A snap.

He woke against a tearing, cutting, churning pressure that felt like someone was trying to expand his anus with an outboard motor.

"Almost done," Dowler said.

That wasn't *too* bad. But still Dowler drilled. Martin squirmed and was held against the gurney.

"Almost done," Dowler said again.

Yeah, right, he told himself.

Gradually, slowly, as if, with a tenuous string, he were removing the Hope diamond from his rectum, Dowler pulled the scope from him.

"Jesus," Martin said.

"All done." He patted Martin gently on the shoulder. "I'll come see you when you're all set up."

Again he was left with the nurse. He dropped his chin tightly against the neck of his gown and tried to sleep.

Afterward, as he sat sipping ginger ale in the outpatient ward, Dowler told him that he was clear and that even his prostate looked good. He shook his hand. "Same time next year?" he said.

"Same time next year," Martin said.

In Hampstead Hospital's lower lobby, lined by stuffed racks of yellowed pamphlets and application forms, Elizabeth registered under the territorial gaze of an elderly receptionist with thinning bluish hair and too-pink lipstick.

"Can't say I've missed it," Richard said under his breath.

"It's so nice of you to come with me." He didn't usually—hospitals upset him—but now she could run six kilometers a day or bicycle eighteen, host dinner parties, meditate for ninety minutes at a time. She had entered the cliché and experienced it from the inside out: she had never felt better in her life.

The receptionist rang up to the eighth floor, murmured Elizabeth's full name, then glanced at her. "You're expected." She waved her on with a steely pen.

Along the hall and in the elevator, she found herself trying not to breathe, as if it were hospitals that made you sick in the first place. Richard held her hand and studied the number of each floor lighting one at a time. She made herself breathe normally.

In the blank office sat Sparks, rising as they entered, a smile sliding onto her face, her hair styled back around each pale ear, a faint luster in each cheek. She'd been cycling in Italy on holiday. Spread before her were the fresh bone scan and stapled pages of lab printouts.

"Was it good?" asked Elizabeth, fumbling with her own Britishy inflection.

Sparks looked at her oddly.

"The holiday."

"Delightful." She grinned reluctantly. "Rather nice. It was good to get the air, and the scenery was fine."

"Was it Tuscany?" Richard asked politely.

She nodded, smiled.

"We've been once," he said.

"I know."

It was rude to ask directly after the results; Elizabeth couldn't help peering at the shiny opaque sheet. Against the white table it was quite black.

"So how are you feeling?"

She blushed, caught in her curiosity. "Great," she said. "I haven't felt this good in years. Running, bicycling. Trips to the health club. Meditation. And my tinctures and vits. I feel quite good."

"That's wonderful." Sparks let the corners of her mouth upturn ever so slightly, and nodded. "I really think you're doing wonderfully, too." She held up the bone scan. "No change, for better or for worse; that's another month of stability. Quite good. And all the blood work is up. You're doing fine."

Beside her, Richard admitted a breath, and reached over and squeezed her hand.

"So I guess we should talk about options," Elizabeth said.

"Alternatives?"

She'd preempted Sparks again. "Yes."

"Well, I was thinking we could try some chemotherapy or increase the hormones."

Elizabeth felt her face falling and pushed it back into place. "I thought you said I was doing fine."

"You're stable," Sparks confirmed. For the first time Elizabeth noticed she was wearing a tiny diamond stud in each ear. Must have a new beau. "The spots on the liver are stable. The spots on the spine are stable. The blood is improved. It's still in your system, Elizabeth."

"Of course, of course. I'm not denying that. I was just thinking I was doing so well that why should I put any more toxins in my system."

"The hormone therapy is what is working for you," Sparks said clinically. "That's quality of life. But to try to destroy the disease with some bold chemotherapy is really your only strategy. Of course," she paused, "the chances are still quite small."

Elizabeth just looked at her, just took in the minute, glittering world of each pinhead of diamond. Understated. Subtle. Expensive.

"Now that you're strong, I think it's your best opportunity."

Elizabeth shook her head.

"Well, you have time. It's not like you have to do it tomorrow."

"I was wondering," Elizabeth said. "I was thinking about going back to work. Not the same job, of course. But, you know, pursuing something."

"What a good idea," Sparks said.

"We were also thinking . . ." Elizabeth threw a sideways glance at Richard; his eyes were open, and he nodded. "We were thinking we might also try for an adoption."

Sparks looked from her to Richard and back again.

"Since I'll never be able to have children—I understand that now—and since I'm stable, we thought we might adopt a child."

"Richard?" Sparks said.

He nodded. "That's what we are thinking," he said.

"I just don't think"—Sparks's ears were turning red from the tips down—"I just don't consider that to be terribly pragmatic."

"But you said—"

"In fact"—she quickly leafed through the test results—"I am certain you'd find the process a quite difficult one in which to achieve an affirmative result."

"Why?"

"Because the health status and projected longevity of the applicant parents are crucial elements in the overall evaluation."

"But I'm stable. I'm not *going* anywhere."

"Even in cases of remission, and yours is not that, it's impossible to proceed without a five-year disease-free case history."

"Five years. I could be dead by then."

She covered her mouth from the horror and truth of what she'd said.

"You're doing fine," Sparks consoled her. "Just keep doing fine. You're surprising all of us."

They already had her damn certificate written out and ready to go. But she couldn't muster the rage. She felt as if Sparks had stuck a hose in her and flooded her veins with everything she was not. Her body. It was so tiring to be conscious of her body all the time. Richard touched her sleeve. His eyes were full. Not that, please not that.

"I guess we'll talk in a month," she said, standing, waiting for the sturdiness. It was somewhere in there, clinging to whatever hadn't been washed away.

"Yes." Sparks smiled patronizingly. "But do call sooner, if you like."

"Thanks ever so much," Richard mumbled.

In the Alfa Romeo convertible—the one she'd treated herself to after a larger than expected bonus—with the top down, she let the wind wash her, the weather golden and dry, stunning. The kind of weather that made you wish you could live forever. Down into the car-exhaust jumble of London they rode, the canyon of buildings rising around them.

"You don't mind the long ride back?"

"Of course not."

"I'm sorry she said what she said."

Elizabeth sighed. At least she had her sunglasses on. At least he wouldn't have to see her like this. "I'll make some calls," she said, smoothing the knees of her pants. "We'll see."

"The States?"

She glanced at him. It wasn't an issue between them. She had decided it was best to continue living in London. She had decided they should stay in their nice new house they'd spent two years and a small fortune to remodel. Refurbish. Restore. Resurrect. They had a scrapbook of how it looked before, how it looked when it was completely gutted out, and how it looked now, as if even now were just another completed phase between then and the future. A scrapbook of their house! She wanted a scrapbook of their children.

"Probably," she said, relieved that their long halt at the light was over, her back sucked into the seat as he roared the last blocks to his office.

He nodded, his face into the wind as neutral as a clock.

She couldn't quite find the door in her brain, but she knew where it was: when they told her that she couldn't, not ever. For five years she and Richard had done calendars and tests and counts and counseling. They hadn't even yet considered in vitro, the cost of it exaggerated by her ambivalence. *What about adoption?* everyone had wondered. She'd dismissed it. Their babies had to come from them. Their babies had to be of them. The self was the center, the sun, the emanator. A child didn't come from the outside. A child came from you. And now, when she'd finally accepted the uselessness of her own *system*, they were going to deny her. She hadn't even miscarried. She hadn't even once been late. She hadn't even ever been certain that she wanted to be a mother. It was

Richard who insisted, Richard who was passionate, and she'd decided, Okay, if it happened. But remove the opportunity, remove her from that side of the world (the healthy side, the do-anything, be-anything, eat-anything side), and she was no longer someone who could think about becoming a mother. She was childless. She was less.

"So here we are," Richard said, the car pulling over at the curb, idling. Oh, she was way below idling. He stroked the back of her bent neck. "I could call in sick."

"No way."

"All right. Then I've got Epiphany until eleven."

"That's fine," she said.

They got out and kissed timidly—or was it tenuously or tentatively? something with a *t*, but something not true—and he shouldered his way through the revolving door into his building, and she got in the car and buckled herself in—as if that mattered—and shifted into gear and pulled from the curb alone.

There is love, she thought. Love is everywhere.

Or was that God?

This endless mixing up of what to think and who she was, of advancing along exactly the right chord to grace, to mercy. Of not being so aware all the time of how fucking alone she was. Of stopping at the stoplight and starting again and taking the circle and pulling over at the storefront and jumping out and making sure she could park there, and running in and plucking out the kind of milk and juice she was supposed to drink and the kind of cheese she was supposed to eat and paying and climbing back in, and taking the right roundabout to the next off-shoot to the next storefront, and picking up the kind of grains and tofu she was supposed to eat and the kind of soup base she was allowed to sip, and in the car making sure not to get hit or hit anyone. And chugging to the next correct shop, and hunting the organic lettuce and radishes and carrots and peppers that she was to eat and dumping them in the boot with the rest of the plastic sacks, and lurching the seventeen stoplights home. And clubbing the steering wheel and lugging the bags in two at a time, remembering to disarm the alarm, and making sure the car was locked and then that she was locked in the house, and stowing the groceries in the proper cabinets, and making room in the fridge, and washing your hands and grinding your wheatgrass and drinking your juice, and passing the living room on your way upstairs, where you couldn't help but notice the couch but avoiding the couch and avoiding the bed, and slipping out of your shoes and opening the thick door of the crib-sized room and landing on your knees, and staring at the picture and bowing and shutting your eyes and then opening them and then shutting them again, then not remembering whether they were supposed to be open or shut—it didn't matter, it was just you in your home, in your farflung, nowhere neighborhood—and beginning or trying to begin, trying to start. Because, anyway, as it had always been since that first day when you'd gotten off the plane from the meeting in Geneva and rushed to that appointment at Hampstead, and there sat the bone specialist with his arms folded across his chest, and you were breathless and in pain from the trip and the cab and just from living, and he said to you as you sat there in the single chair in his ticking office that he was sorry, but he was afraid it was cancer and that it was rather developed, and that was the first time that it opened and you walked through, and you understood for that first time and from here on that you were alone.

At the Halloween parade all the men on the first flatbed truck were dressed as women, but it was the Hot Rod Association, and everyone around Martin laughed and poked one another with their elbows and said, Jeez, would you look at that, there isn't anything those guys won't do. He and Lauren passed Max back and forth so the boy could see as much as he liked, while a block away Sarah sat on the curb with her friends and pretended that at seven years old she didn't have to have a family. Only rarely now did she climb into his arms when he sat watching television or reading on the sofa, and only then when she needed a favor or a treat. Again he walked the one block up to see how she was doing. When she felt him behind her, she turned and mouthed, *Go away. Go. Away.* He walked back down the street alongside a tap-dance troupe from nearby Potterstown busily clacking their castanets amid warm plumes of exhalation, the coaches potbellied, the girls narrow and stiff as posts, the one boy remote and disdainful. They were charming and pathetic, and the people who watched them were charming and pathetic and so, Martin thought of himself, was he, and he tried to feel he had something in common with the migrant workers who hung out in the video arcade at the Wal-Mart and the Civil War reenactors who drove Confederate-decaled four-by-fours and the Girl Scout moms with their GOT JESUS? license plates and the geriatrics who nervously tended their patches of lawn and boxy ranch homes and the clumps of clubby, grubby parents who sucked on cigarettes while waiting for their children to march by so they could scream and hoot and otherwise demonstrate their kinship and affection. It was an odd town, really. Whenever he picked up Sarah from a friend's house he waited patiently at the front door, and whenever someone picked up his or her daughter at Sarah's house, he invited the parent in but the parent always remained just outside. He figured it would take another five to seven years before he and Lauren would be accepted, and yet he wasn't at all sure that this wasn't a town where the people had all decided it was so small that you simply didn't want to get to know anybody any better.

"How is she?" Lauren asked, while Max swatted the air at a rainfall of Tootsie Rolls thrown from the trailing car of Potterstown tap-dance sponsors.

"The same." He wasn't cold and he wasn't bored, but still Martin wanted to ask if they could go.

"Could you hold him for a while?"

He took Max. "Kiss for Daddy?" he whispered. The boy pursed his lips and Martin held his cheek out, and the boy pressed his face to him.

"Fire truck!" His son's body jerked in his arms, hooked by the red blare, and the boy twisted for a better view. Martin could still feel the wet lip imprint on his cheek. It was awful to love your kids so much. It made you fear and dread death in ways you never had before. A friend of a friend who had been medically sentenced to a fast fade had pulled his two little girls from school and spent the last year of his life tied up with them in the living room, soaking them in. At the time Martin, a new father, had condemned the man's selfishness. Now he felt only terrified.

"Martin."

He turned to find the colleague who tormented them and her husband, the dean of retention, smiling obligingly. At his and Lauren's interview dinner this woman had leaned across the table toward them, and cleared her throat. "You need to know we live in a river valley," she'd said in her slight Austrian accent. "Your children will be sick throughout the year with pneumonia and bronchitis." "This is supposed to be a *recruitment* dinner," Ruben had put in, before Martin or Lauren could respond. "Why don't you just tell them we've all grown radioactive from the nuclear power plant?" Now Martin could feel the various elements of his personality shutting down one by one: emotion, honesty, wit. He was all defense. *Witch* was so rooted in his mind as who she was that he could not recall the word for her name.

"Annka," he finally managed. "Arnold." He offered a hand to the dean, a genial guy who had somehow stayed married to Annka for thirty-two years.

"And this is?" Arnold pointed jovially at the back of the boy's head.

"Max." Martin forced the boy around in greeting. "Say hello, Max."

"Fire truck," Max said, wrestling back to catch the last of it.

"So how *are* you, Martin." Annka gave a pointy-chinned smile.

"Fine, fine." He jostled Max, almost using the boy's torso as a shield.

"This is a hard year for you, isn't it," she said keenly. "What with your review and your sister? A lot going on, huh?"

"No," he lied, "not really." They rarely spoke, even though Annka was the other co-chair of the department. If there were no witnesses, she passed them in the halls as if they did not exist.

"Happy to have the bastards back, are you?" Arnold teased.

"The students? Sure, why not."

"That's the spirit." He popped him playfully on the shoulder.

"How *is* your sister?" Again Annka's sharp sympathy was intent on finding something to pierce.

"Stable. She's stable."

"Good. That's really good, Martin." She touched him briefly on the elbow, and he moved back, making sure she did not touch the boy. "And so good to talk to you."

"You, too," he said.

Already they were promenading down the sidewalk arm in arm, their heads practically touching, as they murmured whatever people like them murmur to each other. He held the boy close.

"You all right?" Lauren said, reappearing from wherever she'd hidden herself.

"Let's get out of here," he said.

They set Max in his stroller, his eyes glazing as he chomped on a Tootsie Roll, and headed for the car. Martin and Lauren nodded at David and Cindy Lazlo, who indifferently waved to them, as Martin's throat tightened. In the word *colleague*, he was certain, was an element of the noose, the collar.

"Ride," Max said, when they'd pulled into the garage and he'd hit the button to close them in. He took up Max and carried him inside and upstairs, while in the kitchen he could hear Lauren readying the bedtime snack. Easily—it would be one of those times when Max would let it be easy—he laid the boy on the torn pad of the changing table and took off his shoes and socks, his trousers and diaper.

"Candy," Max sang. "Cannnndeeee." He didn't seem to want any more, he just liked knowing that it was now in the house with them.

"Who's my boy?" Martin said. "Are you my boy? Who's my boy?" He dabbed ointment on his bottom and diapered him, slipped him into pajamas. "Ride?" he offered.

"Want to walk," Max said.

Martin stood him on the floor and the boy ran on tiptoes to the stairs, took each banister spindle in his hand as he stepped his way down, the hair on the top of his head fluffing up with static, his cheeks looking as if they were full of lollipops. Every time Martin looked at him, he just wanted to hold him, hold him, hold him. Let me go, Max was always saying. Lemme go. He was only two, for chrissakes.

"Run around?" Max asked hopefully, his eyes turned up at him at the bottom of the stairs.

"Okay."

Teehee, the boy choked, *teehee,* as they chased through the living room and over a corner of the kitchen and up the front hall past the stairs and into the living room and around again. And again. He kept waiting for Lauren to scold him about getting Max all worked up before bedtime, but she was doing something that he couldn't make out. When he came around the fourth time on the boy's heels, he saw the snack plate on the clean counter but he didn't see her. Then she stepped from the little bathroom, and her eyes were red and she still had a clump of tissue in her hand. Uh-oh. Uh-oh. He pulled up short, the boy instantly squealing, stopping, too, and pulling at his leg.

"What?" he said to her.

"Nothing." She sniffled, gave a sour laugh. "Elizabeth left a message." She swallowed. "She sounded pretty upset."

"All right," he said slowly. It was too late to call her.

"She didn't say anything in particular." She took the sponge and wiped the clean counter. "She just sounded awful."

He looked at her, the boy still squawking. "Could you take him so I can listen to it?"

"You won't sleep," she said.

Outside, someone knocked at the door and Max raced to answer it, and Sarah fell through, laughing, her friend's father red-faced and glowing behind her in the night cold. Martin had enviously smelled booze at the parade.

"Pleasure, pleasure." The father waved at them, as he backed himself into the night. "Kids had a wunnerful time."

"Thank you," Martin and Lauren both called.

"Thank you!" Max said.

Then the door shut, and the two of them were alone in the house with the answering machine and the wound-up, sugar-struck children.

"Go on up and get ready for bed, honey," Lauren said gently.

"Do I have to? Grace's family was gonna go home and stay up and make popcorn and stuff."

"*NOW!*" Martin roared, his own anger stunning him.

Sarah's face flushed and crumpled, and she hustled upstairs. Max whimpered.

"What was that all about?" Lauren wanted to know.

"I want to listen to the message," Martin said quietly, trying to reach for the boy, who swayed immediately away. "She's my sister."

"Okay," Lauren said.

"Now," he said.

But the answering machine was in the kitchen, and Max was in the kitchen and Lauren was in the kitchen, and Lauren set Max in his chair and sat with her back to Martin and began to read, and he wanted to rip out the answering machine and carry it away and slam the door and listen in utter peace. Carefully he undid the wire from the phone and unplugged the machine from the wall and took it into the study, his face furiously blushing, he felt so embarrassed and ashamed and upset. He softly shut the door and plugged the machine in and sat on the futon sofa and set the device on his lap and hit PLAY.

"Bad meeting with Sparks," she was saying, as if she'd begun to talk before the machine had cued the cassette. "I asked her about adopting a child, and she said absolutely not. I can't seem to . . ." Now she was gently sobbing. "I can't seem to have anything I want. I just want a child. Really that's all I want, and Richard is never here." Steadying breaths. "It's all right. I'm all right. Doing fine, really. Call when you can. Bye."

Nothing in particular? He thought that was pretty particular. He yanked the plug from the wall and sat without any red or green light blinking at him. She should just leave Richard, but he could never tell her that. Sometimes you just had to hold on tight as the world fell out from under you and all you had was nothing, nothing. Lie to yourself, he coached his students when they tried to understand a leper colony or female circumcision. Tell yourself that it's the everyday. And then you can see it better. Then you can embrace it and be with it, even if fundamentally you can't accept it. But that advice was more naive than they were.

He and Lauren were observer-participants. Each summer they traveled to a culture to live in it: the basket weavers in the Carolina low country, the snake handlers in the Kentucky hills. But back home every fall, they played their interview tapes and studied their notes and wrote their articles. When Elizabeth had first called to tell him what the bone specialist had found, when he'd sat on the stairs with the phone to his ear and the children swirling through the living room and Lauren gone at the office and she'd said, It isn't good, and he'd felt the stairs through his jeans, felt the air through his shirt, his forehead, he saw it in his head, a wall going up between them, she over there in London, not good, dying, he over here, safe, kids for the moment healthy, wife for the moment healthy, he for the moment healthy, watching that wall go up, shutting her out as if she were just another project—*What exactly are you saying? Can it be managed?*—his voice as formal as a teacher's, the children churning, tugging, wringing him, and finally he tore at the wall. How is Richard? he said. Richard is shattered, she said. And he said, I don't know what to say, I am so sorry, what can I do, I'll do anything, I'll do anything, I'll do anything.

"So what do you want to do?" she said.

They were lying in bed, the room as dark as the inside of his head.

"I don't know."

"We can do it, you know. I can do it. I'd be glad to do it."

"It's not about you being glad to do it. It's not about you being able to do it. It's doing," he grimaced at the cliché he was about to let escape, "what's right. What we ought to do."

"It's what we ought to do," she said.

"Have their fucking baby? She didn't ask us to have their fucking baby."

"We can do it," she replied quietly.

"I don't even know Richard. Richard is still too much of a mystery."

"So you're saying she's going to die." Her voice was bitter, reproachful.

"What else do you expect me to say? Shit, we're all gonna die."

"If we told them we could do it, they'd leap at it."

"It is too fucked up," he said.

"This whole thing," she said, "is fucked up. Maybe if we talked to your mother or Martha . . ."

He groaned. Martha was so surrounded by her own sacrifices that she couldn't possibly attend to anyone else's. His mother?

"We're going awfully fast here."

"It will take *nine months,*" was all she said.

He got up, his bedside scotch glass empty, and went to the window and drew up the shade. It was so late that even the streetlamps in front of the school were off, just the one mustardy light at the corner still lit. From the dark school yard came hollow echoes of practically invisible guys playing basketball. Why the hell were they always there? How often he'd stood here trying to see them, only hearing the thump of the ball and a call or a shout. Mornings, he'd look out at the little kids who got dumped off early each day, waiting under the overhang out of the rain and the dark, or improvising solitary games in the slow sun, or cupping their hands to their mouths, holding momentary clouds to their small, cold faces.

"Martin," she said from the bed, where he could now clearly see the pale shape of her face, the pallor of her bare elbows. "We have to do something."

"All right." He looked up at the empty night sky as if wishing to be struck by anything that could take him outside of himself. "I'll figure it out."

In the morning they stood on the sidelines with all the other parents and grandparents and toddlers and cheered the Possum eight-and-under girls as they kicked the ball up and down the field against the Raccoon team. Max kept trying to run onto the field, and they kept holding him back, his feet striking at their shins. Two fathers, who in their high school football jerseys and baseball caps might have been brothers, lurched in front of them and bellowed happily at their daughters. Then one of them pulled out a dollar bill and waved it.

"If you get a goal, Ashley," he shouted into the field, "I'll take you to McDonald's."

"Hey, Shawna," the other guy hollered, dangling a dollar bill of his own, "score and I'll give you this."

The two men turned to each other and threw back their heads and laughed.

Lauren took up Max, and with Martin they sidled off to where a set of grandparents sagged, sipping coffee as they took in the action.

"There she goes," Lauren said quietly, and she and

Martin watched as Sarah skipped to the ball, hopped at it instead of kicked, and skipped back to position.

"Would you just look at that kid," the old guy next to Martin snorted to the old woman as he nodded at Sarah. "She can't even *kick* the ball. She doesn't even know where she is."

"Why don't you—," Martin started, but Lauren was already pulling him away.

"So she's no good at soccer," Lauren said. "It's no big deal."

"No kidding," he said.

But it was also how Sarah was with the trainer bike and the trainer roller skates she'd asked for and gotten in the summer—she tried them once and then refused to have anything further to do with them. I'm going to be the oldest girl in the world who can't ride a bike, she'd declared. They could never tell whether she just couldn't do much of anything, or she *wouldn't*. Across the field she ran, her arms flapping and her knees knocking into each other. When the whistle blew, Martin felt only relief that the game was over. Once, Lazlo had been out watching his goddaughter play, and Martin told him he was worried about Sarah's development. For a moment Lazlo had watched her silently, then he turned and ran his eyes over Martin. "You know, Marty," he said. "I bet you weren't terribly athletic yourself."

Lauren touched his hand.

"You're letting it get to you," she said.

At the Wal-Mart afterward Lauren let Max and Sarah ride the fifty-cent spaceship while Martin ran in and bought a new cassette for the answering machine. Once home he lifted out the cassette with Elizabeth's message and put it in the accordion file folder with the printed copies of all the e-mails she'd sent him in the last year and all the Internet research he'd done for her and all the info and receipts and tickets for the London trips past and future. Then he went outside and raked while Sarah climbed around the plastic slide set and inside Max sedated himself with television and Lauren cleaned the house. When he was sick of raking leaves, he climbed the breezeway stairs and stood the rake in the garage and walked into the kitchen and took up the phone.

He dialed the work number first because that was where his mother always was. She couldn't escape it, and often it seemed to him she didn't want to—it was the only thing she could trust to be unending.

"Yeah," she said.

"It's me," he said.

"Hello, me. I see you found my hiding place."

"Elizabeth left a message last night."

He swore he could feel her tighten before she even said anything. "And?"

"I don't know. She was having a miserable week." He took a breath. He tried to tell her what Elizabeth had said. Then he said, "Of course Richard was probably at one of his Epiphany things, and that couldn't have helped—"

"She should just move back here," his mother said.

"Well, whatever. I think we need a plan."

"You're not serious," his mother said. "She doesn't want to have any plan from us. She's so good at tending to herself. All that alternative junk she does—"

"You are *so* judgmental," he said.

"Me, judgmental? Me judgmental!" He heard her voice climbing and choking. "How about the fact that she blames me for all of this? If it wasn't how I raised her, it was how I fed her. If it wasn't how I fed her, it was what I took when I was pregnant with her. Don't you call me judgmental—"

"She said that to you?"

"She says that to me every time I talk to her. *Every time.* She says it helps her to let everything out whenever she feels it."

"Oh," he said. He sighed. "So what do you think?"

"What do I think?" his mother said. "Why should it matter what I think? You know what I think. It's too . . . too . . . it's just too impossible. Richard's never there. She's doing only unconventional stuff. I think it's very . . ." She was groping for words. "Very desperate, I guess. What do you think?" she said.

He shook his head, as if she could see him. "I think there are more sides to this than we'll ever know."

"Well, no kidding. There's the other line. Was there anything else?"

"How's Dad?" he remembered to ask, his father's own slow-moving, late-in-life cancer like a kind of overdue bill Martin too easily continued to allow to slip his mind.

"Still with the prostate. I'll talk to you soon."

"Love you," he said.

"Love you," she said.

It was an exchange he had stolen from Lauren's talks with her mother.

"So what did she say?" Lauren asked.

He told her.

"I love the idea of *life* in the middle of all this," she said.

He stared at her.

"I can't help it. I do."

"What about Richard?" he said.

"You sound just like your mother."

His face crimsoned, and he gnashed his lip to keep from screaming at her.

"I'm sorry," she said. "It's just . . . remember how everyone thought their yoga group was a cult, and you had to keep telling them that at least Elizabeth and Richard weren't selling off all their stuff, at least they were still materialistic. It took your family a long time to come around to the fact those guys weren't brainwashed. Now it's the one thing that's saving her."

"I just don't think this idea is very realistic." He was sorry as soon as he'd said it.

"Realistic? What's realism got to do with it?" She went to the fridge and brought out a brick of cheddar cheese and unwrapped it and started chopping it angrily in narrow strips. "Cheese gum!" she shouted into the living room. Max came running, and from upstairs they could hear the race of Sarah's footsteps. "We'll talk about it later," she said.

She had to call him. She didn't want to, but after whatever she'd left on the machine last night, she had

better. What to say? What to say? By the time she got to
the end of wherever she was going, nothing would be left
unsaid. It would all be out in the open and shrunken to
corpuscles of grief and self-pity. Maybe she shouldn't be
allowed to call anyone anymore. Maybe that's what this
was all about, taking her privileges one by one. Was she
so tender that one appointment could crush her so?
Hadn't she learned anything? She switched on the computer and entered e-mail.

"Send me the cassette," she wrote him. "Then we'll
talk."

She hit SEND. He wouldn't get it for another day—he
refused to have e-mail at home—but she liked how relatively immediate it was and how she needn't risk getting
his voice on the phone and having to go further than she
wanted.

She had new mail. Her mother. Martha. Her oldest
nephew. People tapping away at her from all over, tapping their little words of encouragement and companion-
ship. Tap, tap, tapping. Once Martha's son had had each
child from his entire first-grade class send her a get-well
card, and it had made her feel as if she'd already died.
Not yet, she thought. Not yet. At first she'd saved the
cards, with their bright crayon drawings and smiling
faces and stick figures and their endlessly repeated song:
Get well, feel better, get well. Finally she bundled them
neatly and tossed them.

She didn't like flowers either, and she couldn't bear
the smell of champagne.

But she felt great.

Only if she really rooted around inside herself, looking for it, could she find it and know it and understand it. But if she refused to understand, was that merely the mercy of denial, or the thin, impossible chord to wellness?

"Martin." She tapped him another e-mail. "This sucks, sucks, sucks. Oh baby, it sucks."

She hit DELETE and watched it evaporate.

"Those notes I saw you taking during discussion." Annka wagged her pen at him. "Do you do anything with them?"

"All the time," he said. He'd only gone to the board twice, for a total of ten minutes, in a seventy-five-minute class. "I try to create minilectures from the issues they raise. I try to meet them on their own points of engagement."

"I see." She squinted her eyes and offered him what someone who was drunk might have termed a smile. "Could I get a copy of one of those 'minilecture' notes sometime?"

"Of course," he said.

"I mean, if it's no bother."

"No bother at all."

She looked at him as they sat in the empty classroom, all the students long gone. He felt as if he was being kept after. She just looked at him.

"I guess I'd better get going," he said.

"That's fine."

He packed up his briefcase while she sat there. What

did she think behind those glasses, those blank but narrow eyes, under the dark brown sweater set, in that however-the-fuck-old-she-was body? Sometimes he wanted to shake her and shout *I know, I know!* about how she had fought their hire, how she hated them. But you weren't allowed to do that. You weren't even allowed to accost her in the hall and say quietly, Look, I understand you didn't want us here and you don't want us here and you'll never want us here and you have to do what you have to do but we would like it to be—what?—civil, respectful, restrained, fair? Or could he say, Look, we're going to humiliate you before you humiliate us, eviscerate you before you eviscerate us. God, he wanted to tell this blank face, this empty face, this wicked face, At least now I know what the fuck you do with all your time. He snapped the briefcase shut.

"See you." He tried to smile easily at her. "Thanks for coming."

"That's fine," she said.

In his office his hands still trembled. Fear made no sense here, there was so much else to fear. He tried not to think of it. But what was the point of serenity? What was the point of calm? He picked up the phone.

"How was it?" Lauren said, not even bothering to ask who was calling.

"She just sits there." He tried to stop himself, knowing how fatigued she was by his review and how the process awaited her, too. "And then afterward she interrogates me. Do I ever use any other models? Do I ever use any approach besides observer-participant? Do I ever give substantial lectures? Do I ever do anything with the notes I take? Do I wipe myself after I take a shit? Jesus!"

"David Lazlo is leaving Cindy," she said.

"What?"

"I stupidly called Mary again about getting someone into one of his courses for the spring, but it turns out he's not teaching, because he's got somebody out in Kansas and he's taking the spring off to be with her."

"Wow."

"It's been going on for months."

"I thought all that crap he pulled with you was harmless. I thought Cindy was the one who made him tolerable," he said. "Why is everybody falling apart? It wasn't like this in Atlanta."

"Sure it was. We just didn't know about it." Max squealed happily into the phone. "Anyway, Max has a low fever and is on Motrin. Not too listless. Sarah's at Grace's. I'll get her around five. Should we bring you anything?"

"No, not with the fever." He had a bowl of soup waiting for him in the department's fridge, then he taught from six-thirty to nine, then he walked home. "I'll be fine."

"Okay."

He hung up. David Lazlo was a force of nature, all right. Martin feared, envied, and loathed him all at once. Fuck him, he thought. Just fuck him. He clicked on his e-mail. Buddies from graduate school sending their rants from Oregon, New York, Arizona: funds cut, classes underenrolled, tenure tracks dissolved, colleagues knitting nooses in their honor. Elizabeth wanting the cassette back. Martha telling him what kind of computer to buy for Sarah. "I'll call you soon," he wrote Elizabeth.

From four to five his freshman advisees wandered in to review next semester's selections. It was hard for him to believe that he could be allowed to think about next semester, all that time eaten away, all that time survived. When the last of their unprepared faces had left, his head felt punched in from gazing at the computer and trying to determine which course after which course had any empty seats left while the little sons and daughters of bitches had just sat there without any plans or predilections at all, willing him to choose their futures. Outside his window the sun sank. There were still two and a half hours of disengaged and disinterested students to face. At least it made him hold off on his drinking. He felt a little delirious.

He was just getting up to go warm his bowl of soup when the door opened. Instinctively, he shrank from it. The children came giggling in in their pink and green overcoats, followed by Lauren with her arms full of Tupperware.

"I thought . . . ," he said, plucking up Max and squeezing him, setting him down and hugging Sarah, who seemed torn between looking at him raptly and ignoring him altogether.

"Well," Lauren smiled, "we were going out anyway." She set on his desk containers of rice, chicken, and broccoli. Always at least one antioxidant.

"Thank you so much," he said.

"All right, children. Daddy has to work."

She began to herd them back through the door; they were being ridiculously cheerful and well behaved. He just wanted to hold them all. But he had to work.

"Good-bye," he called, his eyes glazing, all that weepy sentimentality lurking just below the surface. If he ever let it out, he'd need a bucket and a mop. "I love you," he said.

"Love you," Max called over his shoulder.

"Bye, Daddy," Sarah said.

The door shut behind them. They were gone.

He looked at all the Tupperware set on his desk. Whenever it was his turn with the children, he never did this. The fact was, Lauren had been nursing him on and off since Elizabeth's diagnosis had seemed to bury him in his own self-pity and fatalism. At first he could not will himself out of bed, and she took the children each morning until one of them *had* to go to work, and he could not remember what he said in class, he couldn't bear to talk on the phone to anyone except Elizabeth, he couldn't bear to do anything except scour the medical books and the Internet for her. In his obsession to do something— anything—when everyone told him there was nothing to be done, he'd taken Lauren for granted. All gone. She was gone. She had taken the children. He had an hour in the darkening boxcar of an office until he had to teach. He was weepy, just weepy. He just loved her. He just loved them. He couldn't make all that love mean anything, because he couldn't express it satisfactorily. Beneath the complaint and the trauma they made him happy and glad and full. Why couldn't he say it, say it all, say it the right way? He swatted at his face. Had to eat. Had to warm the nice food, teach the nice class, walk the nice walk home, kiss her once so primly on the lips because she'd be exhausted as well from the day with Max and the evening with the two of them, and then he'd go and pour the wine and they'd sit on the sofa while he dumbly watched the sports channel or she'd sit in the kitchen catching up on Sunday's news and at eleven or eleven-fifteen, after two glasses for her and three or four glasses for him, they'd trudge upstairs, check on the children, slide into their pajamas, brush their teeth, floss, turn out the light, turn once groggily to each other and kiss a last perfunctory or sometimes tender kiss, and drop into sleep. And he'd never say it. He'd never express it. Today would become another missed day in a year of missed days, of climbing out of bed into the daily slog, of projecting energy into the void, of the endless *tick* against the endless *tock,* when he couldn't say, when he hadn't said, when he needed to say, how much he felt her.

I am keeping a journal, she wrote, so that no one will have to hear how afraid I am, how being afraid of death is not good enough, how you can't give in to it and let it rule you, how exhausting it is, how careful you have to be in everything you ever do. I am keeping a journal only when I want to keep it and I am keeping it away from anybody else—even Richard, even Martin, even Martha—

and when it's done and I am somewhere else, it will be like a rock that never existed and no one will have to even know how awful it is and no one will have to know what it means to die and why it should matter how they die, how they take it, because I will not be the sick sister, I will not be the sick wife, I will not be the sick daughter. I will not, I will not, I will not. I will not be mad and I will not be miserable and I will not be afraid and I will not be pitiful. I will follow my God because that is part of whatever the healing can be, and I will not think only of the numbers and I will not hold back what shouldn't be held back and I will be. The difference being the difference between being and doing. I will be. I will do whatever can be done, but I will also be.

Yesterday he finally called. We talked about what the children were doing and we talked about the usual shit about Mom and we talked about what it means to complain, how complaining is okay, how everyone complains, how everyone has something to complain about. I could hear him getting tired and I said, "I don't want to drag you down with me," and he said, "You're not." But I heard it in his voice and I lied and said, "Look, I've really got to run. There's someone at the door." And I could hear the relief in his voice as he tried to offer up a resigning "okay." We hung up. He is the one I am closest to and I've told him that and not to tell anybody else that, and he said of course not but why does it matter who I'm closest to? Why am I being like this? Why am I pitiful? Why am I doomed? Why *can't* matter.

Maybe I won't write in this journal again.

———————

Was that really her? She'd always distrusted journals, she'd always felt they kept you from living, that while you wrote in them life went by, and you rose afterward still heavy from seeing inside yourself, and you were slow to catch up. She didn't have time for slow.

In the kitchen she put away spoons and bottles, hearing the hollow echo of her tending to herself. When they'd first gotten beyond the shock, Richard had suggested a dog. *A dog.* As if she were blind. As if she were an old woman living alone looking for any constant company to extend her time. He was only thinking aloud. A dog wasn't it. Every now and then Martin or Martha would dare, Are you sure you don't want to move back? She didn't want to interrupt Richard's and her life like that. She'd only move back if she was afraid. She refused to be that afraid. He'd murmured about it again on the phone last night. No, she'd said, I don't think so.

I have to run, she'd said. There's someone at the door.

She shut the journal and winced with pain as she pulled on an overcoat. For a while she stood under the dangling crystals and took deep breaths. All she felt was a new pain blooming in her shoulder.

At the spa she walked the treadmill for twenty minutes, stretched for twenty minutes, swam for twenty minutes, and then sat in the juice bar watching the sun on the wooden tabletop, dozing and then waking to the low grind of the blender, drinking two glasses of apple-ginger juice. At noon the bar began to fill with corporate exercisers in their ironed white togs. She drove to a row of clothing shops and found a pale blue sweater to go with Richard's eyes. She had to keep holding it up to the light to make sure, as if her eyes were thinking of failing. By two-thirty she had popped another fifty vits and made it in time to art therapy. Four men and five women, all sick in ways she didn't want to hear about, sat in a straggly circle, huge easels in front, oversized sheets of paper shielding them from one another.

"I want you to paint," Marge said, looking at them and then looking out one of the many-paned windows that brought in the last of the day's northern light, "something from your own history, something that was so deep inside you and so much where you'd been and who you were and even who you'd become, that sometimes— maybe even often—you'd forgotten it was there. Until just before now, when news of your own struggle hit you, and you began to work at unpacking yourself and putting you back together, to get it right, and there was this thing that you'd somehow forgotten about, and you understood it was a most essential piece. What is that thing?"

Elizabeth started with pink, which became pale red, black for hair and eyebrows and even lips, blue for the dress, pale red for the legs, black for the shoes. What kind of shoes were they? She could only remember her mother in fat, white high heels, but it was too late for white. She didn't want to make up anything. She wanted it to be true. She added blue to the black. Navy blue heels. Now another face, white outlined in black, tufts of hair at the ears, a line of mouth in pale red, black-outlined neck. She could not remember what her father wore. Yellow, she wanted it to be yellow, but it wouldn't be. Sometimes he had worn suits. Dark suits. When was it worst? When he didn't have to wear a suit? That didn't seem right. Blue for the legs: jeans. Red and yellow and black for a plaid shirt, what he wore when he helped them up to the roof to claw leaves from the gutters. White for sneakers.

"Your father and mother," Marge said easily.

Elizabeth nodded.

She pointed at the woman. "Your mother's that much larger?"

Elizabeth shook her head, but she had drawn her mother at nearly twice the height of her father.

"Well," Marge said. "It's a lot of red and black and blue."

"Pretty obvious, huh?" She pathetically wiped a tear out of the corner of her right eye.

"I don't know. You have a brother and a sister, too, but they're not in here."

"No."

"You're not going to put them in."

"No."

"Are you finished?"

Elizabeth shook her head.

"I hope I haven't said too much." Marge eased on to the next student.

Elizabeth dipped into the black paint and began in the background, almost blotted out by the oversized figures, the structure of a house, five windows wide, the furthest right over brick, the middle two above a porch, the two left above downstairs windows. The porch had a black roof. The roof above the second floor was all black, the chimney white. In the windows she wanted to paint their small faces, but they were hiding, terrified, the house soon to rock with their mother's voice as she spied the broken kitchen window and pounded up the stairs. I'm going to let you have it! she shouted. I'm *really* going to let you have it. How old were they then—nine, seven, and three? Don't, they would beg, as she swung the belt. Don't.

I'll never know, Elizabeth couldn't help thinking as she watched the painting of her mother, I'll never know what kind *I* would have been.

Late at night he sat with the cats at the bar in the basement, sipping another glass of wine and taking one-shot hits of marijuana. Upstairs, in the bedroom, she waited. If he held out long enough, she'd be asleep. Tomorrow was *her* teaching day. He'd only have Max, laundry, bills to pay, dishes, Sarah to amuse after school, dinner. He could walk around in a fog if he had to. Do you really need to do that? Lauren had said when he slid toward the basement.

The bar—which they hadn't touched since moving in—had a mirrored back bolted onto black glitter board. THE CAPTAIN'S RULE IS LAW, declared a sign nailed to one of the cabinet doors. COCKTAIL HOUR ABOARD: 7:00 A.M. TO 6:59 A.M. DAILY AND SUNDAYS. He swiveled on the pink stool. He loved this bar. He pushed himself off and reached behind the counter and brought out a pack of light cigarettes. He and Elizabeth used to shoplift LifeSavers together from the Acme on Woodbine, when he was six and she was ten. In a hideout by the creek, they'd re-count their loot and divide it. Ten years later they planned an elaborate tour of Europe together. They took a train all the way from Germany to Greece, boarded a ferry to an island, climbed steps to a white villa, purchased rooftop accommodations for fifty cents each. When he was in college in New Jersey, he visited her once every few weeks in New York, where they ate and drank in tapas bars and he pretended that he liked her friends from work. One New Year's Eve they dressed up and went to all the parties, told everyone they were each other's dates. That kind of crap.

Before he was born, an uncle whom he would be named after lay dying of cancer, his brain growing mishmashed. Close the venetian blinds, he'd ask, when he meant: Turn off the television. His wife, sweet faced, utterly gentle, attended him. They were childless. "A man as sick as I am," he managed to say once, quite clearly, "does not tell his wife his thoughts." What did that mean? Martin now wondered. Regret? Bitterness? Hatred? What would be left between him and Elizabeth if he stood beside her a last time? Would all the accrued memory feel something like mercy, or was mercy the release from exhaustion and pain? Couldn't denial—the instinct that even as you slipped under you still might emerge again—be merciful? Was grace acceptance or wishful thinking? He wanted to *know*. He couldn't know.

He drew on the cigarette, in the mirror watched himself fill with smoke, then clouded the basement. The cats snarled and chased each other over stalagmites of toys. "*Mel*," he warned. "*Chance.*" They ignored him. "Are cats smart?" his mother once asked him, after a weekend of baby-sitting while he and Lauren had visited London. "I mean, they don't come when you call them." "I don't know," he'd said. "Well, I don't think they are," she'd said. He'd scooped up Max and sat at the kitchen table. They'd arrived only a few minutes ago. "Daddy," Max said, "I miss you." "I missed you, too," he said. "I missed you terribly." "Daddy," Max said, "I miss you tewibly, too." The boy put his damp face into the hollow of Martin's neck and rested there.

Now he crushed out the almost-whole cigarette and looked at himself in the bar back. Past midnight and he was alone. Past midnight, and upstairs she slept. In London another day had gone by, there was another day to get through. He couldn't imagine what it was like.

Y o u k e e p trying, is what you do. You listen to the numbers when they're good, and ignore them when they're bad. You do flushes and decide that the pieces and chunks and stones in the toilet bowl afterward are the *it* of it coming out. You let the shamans and healers take you wherever and however you can. You lie to yourself. You tell yourself the truth. You touch his hand whenever you can, you follow the crease of his collar to the soft belly of his throat, you crumple his earlobes between your fingertips whenever he comes in late from a course or a meditation and you tell him how glad you are that he is growing in all this. You get up every morning and go after it. You try not to call everybody all the time. You stay within yourself. You get out of yourself as much as possible. You deny the self. You are all self. You swim in a flood of meditation, constructive reading, and organic vegetables. When he's left you for another night of Epiphany or yoga and you can hide it from yourself, you sneak a bite of chocolate, a slice of steak, a dab of pâté, a sip of wine, hours of television. On the Internet you surf the humor sites and send a selection every Monday to the e-mail list of your mother, brother, sister, cousins, old colleagues, friends. You crawl into bed every night and hunt for pockets of energy that you forgot to burn. You lay awake long after he has fallen asleep. You use the toilet six or seven times. You wonder what God will look like. You listen, breath held, for the phone to ring and then you will answer it and the voice on the line will say whatever you most need it to say. There's been a mistake, and you don't have what they told you you have. Or, You're going to be a mother. Or, I love you, we love you, everyone loves you. Or, You can rest now. Go ahead now, rest. And then you will. Although for a few minutes after the phone still hasn't rung, your heart will beat too rapidly, and sweat will trace its way along the lifelines of your palms and in the creases under your knees. And then you will. You will rest. It won't be a rest like the rest you used to have, if you can remember what that felt like. It will be a rest from which you will wake unrested and hoping to discover that it's all been a dream, just a mistake, just a nightmare. The dream is the tremor of the *it* in you, and the sleep around the dream is as shallow as the bed you are in, and you wake—what?—almost disappointed to find that you are still alive and that you haven't arrived at some new, daring, dazzling, endless world.

Later still, he found himself swaying in the kitchen, feeling for the phone, opening the refrigerator and dialing in its light. Her voice. How are you's. Questions about the kids, how she missed them and loved hearing stories about them and would he please please please send some pictures or a video. Stuff they always said.

"I want you to know we're thinking about having a baby for you," he heard himself say. He'd had more than he could count and he looked at his near-empty glass, puzzled by what he'd just offered.

"You've got to be kidding," Elizabeth said incredulously.

"Isn't it——" He gulped the rest of the drink. He'd forgotten he'd switched to vodka. Not much resistance there. Maybe if he'd chosen scotch he could have shut himself up. "——What you want." He fucking wished he could put the phone down and yet he noticed how exhilarated he was beginning to feel.

"What?" she said. "What?" She lowered her voice.

"A baby," he said, his voice brimming and spilling over. "Lauren wants to. You know. Have it for you." He reached for the bottle. "It's not like we could adopt it for you and give it to you. But we figured, you know, with Richard . . . Lauren could . . . the whole artificial thing. We're thinking about it."

"But I never asked you," she said. "I mean this is fantastic, it's so selfless. Idealistic. Overwhelming. Definitely an out-there idea. But. Can I speak to her?"

"She's asleep." His words were slurred. "They're all asleep."

"You're very weird," she said.

"Just thought I'd let you know."

"But you are so good to me," she said.

"I know."

"I know you know, but I need to say it."

"Umm."

"Should I tell Richard?"

"Just that we're thinking about it. Just tell him that."

"Call me tomorrow, okay?"

"Okay."

He hung up and staggered up the dark stairs. What had he done? What had he done? Boy, that was stupid. Boy, was it dumb.

"I heard you," Lauren said.

She was sitting up in bed.

"You oughtta be asleep. It's after two."

"Now we have to," she said, "if she wants to. If they want to. Which is fine with me. But now we really have to."

"Okay, okay." The room was turning a little. So that was how much he'd drunk. He was a drunk idiot. "Can I get some sleep? I just want to sleep." He couldn't even get out of his clothes, he was that tired.

"It's fine with me, you know," she said again. He felt her touch him on the shoulder. "You knew I wanted to." "Uh-huh." Now his face was in his pillow. Now she'd be quiet. Now he could get a little sleep. And after, he could start hating himself.

ANTHROPOLOGY

So you're going to do it?" Martin's mother said, her voice filled with disbelief and even perhaps awe.

"I guess so." He heard his own hesitation and tried to ignore it. "I mean, I said we would. Of course we will."

"Well," she said. She paused, swallowed. Every time he talked to her on the phone she seemed to be eating. She swallowed again. "Even if it doesn't happen, I'm proud of you two."

That was unbelievable. That was unheard of. In his entire life he'd only heard that once from his parents— from his father, when he and Lauren had bought the house. That had infuriated him, it was so . . . so full of a kind of middle-class mind-set. This time was different. It scared him.

"Of course, I also think you're crazy," she said.

"Thank you," he said.

He set the phone down and sat at the black desk in their bedroom, in the corner between the windows. Outside, the A.M. kindergarten was having their recess. He knew when the first grade was out and the second grade and the third grade, when Mrs. Lowe ran other outdoor activities, what time of the day she climbed up onto the flat roof and threw down all the lost balls, when she began to gather the bases and bats and hoops and put them in the metal pushcart to wheel inside. Often when Sarah's class was out, he would watch by tipping back his chair. Some days she stood flat against the brick wall and sucked on the loose strands of her hair, other days she ran around aimlessly, unable to decide which group to join or unable to find a group that would have her, and sometimes she led her own pack of kids and he was happy for her. He couldn't remember when he began hating recess, when he saw how slow and uncoordinated he had become compared to everyone else, when he wasn't growing as fast. Lauren had told him she'd been the same. The whistle blew and the A.M. kindergarten raced to their yellow-paint marks at the curb.

He turned to see one of the cats gnawing at the corner of the bed frame.

"Git!" he shouted. It scampered. Hard to tell which one it was, they both looked exactly the same, one the mother, the other the son. But the son was twice as large. He wondered if they had sex. He and Lauren hadn't, since his declaration.

Then the phone rang, and it was the hospital calling, apparently to tell Lauren that Richard's stuff had arrived. "Just have her call us," the woman said for the second time, after Martin had prodded again for the reason for her call. He left a message on Lauren's voice mail.

"Richard."

It was her calling him. It was him calling himself.
Wasn't he asleep? Didn't he have to get in early tomorrow? Didn't he have another evening course?

"Richard."

It was her. "What?" he said. "What is it?"

"I am," she said. "I am feeling better. A lot better."

"I know." He reached and held her hand. She was
sweet. She was brave. She still should have told Martin
and Lauren about the last tests. They should know. They
should know everything if they were really going to inject
his swimmers in her. Hard for him to believe, actually.
Maybe they wouldn't. They probably shouldn't.

"I'm going to call that guy tomorrow," she said. "Or
today." She laughed. "Whenever."

"What guy," he yawned. It was impossible to keep up
with all the people she had to see and all the people
there remained to see and the pools and pools of
unknown people that she hadn't even dipped into yet. It
was quite a little industry, all these people. Not that
they weren't good. Even the guy with the pendulum
who dowsed their house pinpointed the exact reason
why all the food molded on the western quadrant of the
kitchen counter. Elizabeth found and went to only the
good people, only the people who charged a small fortune, only the people who weren't covered by their
insurance. Not that that was a problem. It wasn't a
problem. It was just making them skint, was all. Now he

was waking up. He didn't want to know what time it was. It wasn't time.

"That ayahuasca *guy*," she said forcefully.

"Oh." He was all for that guy—he was offering some kind of medicinal hallucinogen. It sounded kind of fun. It sounded like it could be an opening. He was all for openings. None of this closing-you-down nonsense. There were lots of openings left. She still looked pretty great. Just a bit of a slide here. "I'm all for that," he said.

They squeezed hands.

"I'm afraid I really have to get some rest, sweets," he heard himself murmur. "Epiphany again tonight, you know."

"If we all go through with this," she said, "which room do you think should be the nursery?"

"Whichever you like."

"Orange or yellow or peach?"

"Don't know."

"I think I want to get up," she said.

"Sweets." From his point of view it was just too soon, yet here she was, keeping him up another night, or dragging him from sleep, or whatever was happening. She had to speculate—which kind of nappies, which kind of formula, which kind of ointment, which kind of changing table, which kind of crib, which kind of carpet, which kind of window dressing, which kind of wall clock, which kind of night-light. He'd always wanted a child, and when he saw that they couldn't, he'd wanted them to have as much comfort and pleasure as possible. Now there was little of either, and they might after all have that baby. It was actually kind of exciting. Cripes. "Sweets, I can't do this again," he said.

"I'm not asking you to." She was already out of bed and pulling on her robe, the one her sister had given her for the wedding shower in New York. He'd thought those were awful days, in that tiny condo with the sole window onto a brick wall. He hadn't known what an awful day truly was. "I'll be in the kitchen," she said.

When he finally got up and jammed himself into his slippers and pulled on a sweater and sighed down the stairs, it was just past four o'clock and she was sitting at the kitchen table moving around cut-up pieces of paper on a larger sheet of paper. One of the pieces was marked CRIB, another DRESSER, a third CHANGING TABLE, a fourth ROCKER, a fifth PLAY TABLE.

"What are you doing?" he said.

She barely looked up at him. "The nursery."

When she finally did turn from her work, he saw her skin was again tinging yellow and the wells around her eyes were even deeper and darker.

He touched her shoulder. "Look," he said, "you need to take care of yourself."

"I know," she said.

"You need to sleep, Elizabeth."

She shrugged off his hand. "I don't want to sleep too long," she said. Her shoulders shuddered. She moved a piece off the sheet of paper entirely. "I'm so tired," she whispered. "Nearly all the time. I need to *do* something."

He rubbed her back.

"Really clean out my system." She was teary.

"Okay," he said. "Okay." He knelt and put his arms around her, and she rested her head on his shoulder. "Whatever you want."

In the late afternoon, from work, he called their house. Lauren answered.

"I . . . I wanted to thank you guys. It's really wonderful what you're thinking of doing," he tried.

"Richard? How are you? Your—your package arrived yesterday," she said.

"It's actually a little bit of a mess," he said.

"What? What's going on?"

"There's something you both need to know, that Elizabeth couldn't bring herself to tell you on the weekend. Her last tests weren't terribly good. Just now she hasn't been feeling her best."

"I think we knew that."

"She'll probably have to go away for a while. She's got some things she needs to work out."

"And?"

"Well, you know, if you want to delay your . . . you know . . . I'm sure that would be fine by her."

"Do you not want the baby?" she said softly.

"Of course we want the baby. It's just, we can't be hiding anything from you, is all."

"Don't worry about me," she said.

"I'm not. We're not." He ought not to have called, but he was glad to hear how dead set on it she was. "What you're doing, it's remarkable. Wonderful. It's a real gesture of . . . love. I guess I should run. Work and all. Thanks."

"We'll call soon," she said.

He replaced the phone, looked at the computer monitor. He really should have said something more. Mr. Not-Terribly-Present (wasn't that how Elizabeth's mother referred to him?) getting a last go at lineage. The little in-law baby. Nothing too horribly wrong about that. He should have told Lauren something about all the ways they had tried to get pregnant, but Elizabeth had said it was better just to let it play out, that this was a real chance. Lauren would probably think he was pushy. She'd probably think he was getting cold feet. She'd probably think he was wary of being more tied to that whole uptight family. So odd how it was all about reproduction and nothing about sex. So odd how they'd spent a small fortune trying to determine their own way in this, and then these guys parachuted in with hormones and a turkey baster and suddenly it was a whole new day. So odd how involved and outside of it he was.

It was his teaching night, and after the artificial insemination procedure at the hospital, she alone fed the children and bathed them and read to them and put them to bed. Max called for another story, then called for water, then called for a half cup of dried Cheerios. Sarah lay in bed for an hour reading, and at lights-out continued to read in the dark.

"How do you do that?" Lauren asked her, standing in the doorway.

She shrugged. "I just do."

When Sarah was finally asleep, Lauren poured herself

a glass of wine—the doctor said it would have no effect—
and set it on the counter, then gathered the cats and carried them one by one into the basement. Sometimes at
night she could hear them all the way from the bedroom,
knocking over piles of toys and colliding into the wood
paneling. She shut herself in with them and went to the
basement bathroom to refill their water dish. When she
turned the water on, the faucet shot up and chunked
against the rafters and the water sprayed from the open
line. She was instantly soaked, and the water did not
stop. She snatched up the faucet and through the rush of
water tried to screw it back into place. It shot up again
and ricocheted off the ceiling. Below the sink the only
valve was connected to the toilet bowl, and when she
turned it, it did nothing. Now she was standing in several
inches of water, and it had spilled out into the rest of the
basement. She shouted up the stairs, hoping that Sarah
would hear her, but no sound came from the upper
floors.

She ran up in the sopping clothes and got a flashlight
and brought it back down to the basement and opened
the dark stall that held the furnace and the water heater.
Out shot a furry, four-legged thing, and before she could
swing something at it, it raced across the floor, over the
stairs, past the lazy or tongue-tied cats, and up into the
house. She strangled back her outrage.

"Where is it, exactly," she muttered to herself, her
voice nearly calm, as she waved the flashlight. At the
base of the water heater, she found what looked like a
good prospect. She turned the tap until she couldn't turn

it any more, then came out from the stall and shut the door. The basement sink was still. Despite all the water the sump pump had yet to kick on. In the kitchen, she dialed the first plumber she could find and made an appointment, searched halfheartedly for the mouse that the cats apparently had no interest in, and got the mop and bucket, took a gulp of wine, and shut herself down in the basement. At least Martin would be home soon. It was nothing, really. She mopped and wrung and emptied, mopped and wrung and emptied. When the upstairs door opened, she was distractedly slaving away.

"What happened?" he said gloomily, not even kissing her.

She told him.

"This fucking basement," he said. "Did you call the home-warranty guys?"

"No." She felt a pang of fury.

"Well, we have to use *their* plumber. Otherwise we'll get charged for this shit. And I have no idea what to do about the fucking mouse."

"Do you have to talk like that?"

He looked at her.

"I was here with no one to help me, and I did the best I could. For god's sake, can't you just shut up and give me some sympathy?"

"I'm sorry," he said blankly. He picked up the second mop and started to work. She'd told him to shut up. You were never supposed to tell him to shut up. It was the one thing that hurt him easily. It was how his mother had scolded him growing up. Shut up, she'd said. Just shut up. Over and over and over again. Lauren couldn't look at him as she mopped. Upstairs, the phone rang and neither of them moved to answer it. The machine clicked on, and she hoped it would be a hang up. In her wet clothes she shivered. It was amazing how he could take any situation when she deserved a little sympathy and understanding and turn it around in an instant to where he deserved it more. He brought any guilt out in you. How the hell did he do that? She shouldn't give in. She shook her head. Her face was hot.

"I'm sorry," she said.

All week she attended morning conferences on the Inner Child, and in the afternoons she ground up wheatgrass, carrots, beets, ginger, apple, tomato, banana, any root or herb that had any medicinal value, and juiced and juiced. On Thursday and Friday she took a series of flushes and topped them off with a colonic. She felt terrific.

When the ayahuasca guy arrived at two on Saturday, she was surprised and disappointed to discover that he was white. He was expensive. Richard had removed the table and the television from the living room and drawn all the shutters, and she and he smiled uncertainly at the man while he slipped off his shoes in the hall and brought his rug and his bag into the empty living room. Richard had lit candles.

"We light them later," he said. Richard nodded and went around snuffing them out. The man undid the rug and unrolled it on the living-room floor, took a mug from his bag and poured from a thermos the ayahuasca-soaked water into it.

"You must concentrate, of course," he said. "That is virtually everything."

They each sat on a side of the rug, one side empty.

"A few breaths," he said.

They breathed. She could hear her and Richard's empty stomachs whining. Now they passed the mug and swallowed a bitter drink. It could get inside, under the nothing, and it would bring the spirit out and you could see who you were, who you could be, who you would be. The principle was not to define any shape, he said. He chanted. They chanted. The room grew darker, and they breathed. At the window there was a wind. The candles grew brighter. There were so many positions within the position of sitting. There were no limits in any definition of you. There was breathing without sound. There was feeling the hairiness of the rug but not feeling it. There was his white face that might not after all be white. There were weeks in hours. There was counting without numbers. The candles lingered as if time were not an issue, and that could be true, too, that it was now beyond time. You had your own reference and it was not time; it was elemental. There was love. There was peace. There was an emptiness so sorrowful it was filled with joy. Beyond the body and beyond time were only purity, simplicity, truth, and more emptiness, and the emptiness was like the inside of a diamond, a clarity of being nothing but itself and impossible to see, and it was beautiful and it was you.

And just like a diamond, you could not be broken down into nothing, because you were always something and the something was the emptiness and the emptiness was you.

Then, in the night, he pulled everything back into his bag and rolled up the rug and let himself out, and she and Richard still sat in their positions that weren't positions, in the cleared living room now empty of him.

She wanted to say so much, and yet she knew that if she did it would ruin it for him, and besides it was clear from the stillness that she was not supposed to.

Wow, she might have said.

Wow, he might have said.

Now what?

"I love this place," Ruben said as they took seats at a window table at Rosita's. "Don't you just love this place?

"It's a great place." Under the fluorescent lights Martin looked at the laminated menu. He never went out for lunch, but Ruben had insisted it was part of the review process.

"So how's it going? How are things?"

"Fine," he said.

"Annka torturing you?"

"Of course."

"That bitch," Ruben said. "But you've got to know she has absolutely no ultimate influence. I mean, look, we *were* able to hire you. How's Lauren holding up?"

"Good. Good."

Rosita's brother came and they ordered. Ruben

drummed his fingertips on the Formica table. Martin leaned back in the vinyl booth and stretched. They watched the brother drift around in the kitchen.

"This was where we interviewed you two," Ruben said.

"Yup." On the television perched up in the corner, two overly made-up characters were looking at each other with glistening eyes, talking softly in Spanish. Then the woman's voice rose and she slapped the man, and he stood there touching his cheek.

"Julia isn't doing too well," Ruben said. "A week out of rehab she was walking around town slugging painkillers, and I had to put her back in. A total fucking free fall."

Martin made himself look at Ruben. He'd had no idea. "I'm sorry."

"Your lawyer couldn't take the case. He's been representing the director of fucking human resources of the company in her divorce." He shook his head. "Have you seen Lazlo around?"

"Not since—"

"That guy is going to go down in a ball of flame. I've been sending him e-mails, leaving messages. Nothing."

Their iced teas came and they sipped them.

"I wouldn't care," Ruben said, "except for Cindy, of course. I've known her as long as I've known him. She's my best friend. Besides David. You haven't heard from him at all?"

"Not a word."

"That fucker. I tell him that in my e-mails. I say, You fucker, you are fucking up your life, what is the fucking matter with you?" The iced tea splashed from his glass as he angrily set it down. "I write him that I know he is destroying himself out of his own self-love, but that doesn't mean he can destroy other people. That fucker."

"That's being direct," Martin said.

"It's what all this shit with Julia has taught me. Be direct. You *suspect* something, be direct. You *see* something, be direct. You *know* something, be direct. Fire away."

"I feel that—"

"Of course you do."

They sat there looking at each other.

"So what do *you* want to say?" Ruben said.

"About what?"

"Tell me about your sister."

"I'd rather—"

"Come on!"

"She's fine." He saw Ruben staring at him. "Okay, she's not fine."

"Why are you so obsessed with her? Is she your only sister?" Martin shook his head. "Your favorite?" Martin nodded. "You feel guilty? You feel fearful for your own mortality? This thing is tearing you up!"

"Come on, Ruben." Martin sipped his iced tea.

"It's just like this thing with Julia. I know that's a stretch, but I know you can see it. Right?"

"Sure," Martin said.

Rosita's brother set their enchilada plates in front of them. *Finally,* Martin thought. Ruben picked up his fork.

"Fuck all this medical crap," he said.

"Yeah," Martin said.

"And fuck all this legal crap. And fuck all this work crap. And fuck all this betrayal crap. Am I right?"

"You're right," Martin said.

"That's what I like about you, Martin. You always agree with me."

Martin lifted his fork. "You're my fucking boss, Ruben."

"Right," Ruben said. He started eating. "Once you have tenure, that kind of goes away."

"I know," Martin said. "Thank god."

They ate, Ruben chewing his food loudly and swallowing loudly and gulping his iced tea loudly, as if he thought Martin were a deaf person who needed to know that he was indeed eating and drinking.

"You must have *some* questions," Ruben said, wiping his lips and beard with a handkerchief.

"Yeah," Martin said, setting down his fork. "How the hell do you get rid of a mouse?"

At the Y, Lauren peeled Sarah from her clothes and helped her into her swimsuit, then sat at the window in the lobby and watched her and the other Seals dive and swim. Sarah's braid swung as she hustled along the apron of the pool, and she shivered and clasped her hands tightly under her chin, as if she were praying.

"She looks pretty good out there," Cindy Lazlo said, sliding casually in beside her, even though they hadn't seen each other in months. She pointed with a thin finger. "I bet she'll make Porpoise by spring."

Lauren hunted for something to say. Even *How are you* was loaded. "As long as she keeps at it," she tried.

"That's right," Cindy said. "You guys are crazy to be worried about her."

The swim teachers threw out two long, thin rafts, and the kids romped on them and swung at one another with yellow foam-core noodles.

"This is the only part she likes," Lauren said.

"I want you to know I'm doing great," Cindy said. "I know people at the college must be talking, and I just wanted you to know that." Her face was as pale and gaunt as ever, and her red hair was thin and wild.

"I'm glad," Lauren said. "You look great."

"I had a party at the house last night, and there was nobody telling me which CD to play and which wine to serve. You know what I mean?"

"I know."

"I bet you do," Cindy said. "We all do. How's Martin's sister?"

"Oh." She gazed at the kids lining up to climb from the pool. "It's unspeakable."

"I'm so sorry," Cindy said.

"Thank you," Lauren said.

"Who knows why anything happens to anybody?" Cindy smiled at the window. "Who knows why people do what they do to each other? Maybe it's all fate." She turned to look at Lauren. "Health. Love. Whatever happens."

"Maybe," Lauren said, although she hated when people tried to equate anything they were going through with what was going on with Elizabeth.

"Maybe everything is fragile and arbitrary," Cindy

said. "That's all I'm saying. But of course I really don't believe that. I guess I don't know what to believe. What do you think Martin's sister believes?"

"I think she wants to believe in the possibility of anything," Lauren said. "That's why she tries everything. I used to think that people who went to Mexico for laetrile or coffee enemas were just deluding themselves." She bit her lip. "Well, I don't anymore." She rose from the chair and nodded toward the dressing room down the hall. "It's really great to see you again."

"You, too."

"Will you be here next week?"

"They switched the aerobic schedule. I'm actually here this one time just to see you."

"Oh." Lauren blushed. "I should have called."

"Don't sweat it." Cindy stood and scanned the kids filing from the pool. "We're all going through something."

As Lauren hurried down the hall, she saw Sarah still dog-paddling toward the ladder, her braid wriggling in the water, and she felt as if she were dog-paddling right with her.

In the dressing room Sarah stood shivering by her locker.

"Okay, sweetie, suit off," Lauren said. There were other mothers around, herding their daughters in and out of the shower, reorganizing plastic bags of shampoo and combs and clothes. Sarah pulled off her suit and ran on tiptoes into the shower. Lauren got the water the right temperature and handed her the bar of soap. "Wash up and then you can shampoo," she said. Water sprayed lightly against her jeans. She stood at the wall in the fog of the shower. She had fifteen minutes to get her dressed and out the door, to race over to campus to pick up Martin on the way to picking up Max. Then home, dinner, bath for Max, bedtime snacks, bedtimes. And when the kids slept, Christmas lists. She had to hunt in the catalogs because the town's stores sold only Civil War souvenirs, and because she bought from the catalogs, they now received twenty or thirty a week, and they sagged in overweight piles on the kitchen shelves, and every time Martin tried to throw them out she had to stop him. She wasn't done yet. She had twenty-five people to shop for, and she never knew what she was going to get them until she found it.

"Okay," Sarah called from the mist. "Shampoo, mommy."

Through the spray she handed her the bottle. "All right," she pleaded. "Please hurry."

Then she felt a rush, and she thought, Oh, oh.

"Honey, I'll be right back."

In the dark, damp stall, she sat on the toilet and felt the blood leave her. Maybe the whole idea was stupid; maybe she was just a stupid idealist. Martin's family called her *Miss* Lauren, as if she were a fragile, arrested presence, but they were the ones who were counting up their time and their money, trying to figure out how much Elizabeth could have. "She's the one who decided to stay in London," Martha had said. "If it were me, I would have just come home and gone for the chemo blast." Elizabeth just wanted her life. Couldn't they see that? Couldn't anybody see that? Everything was too bad, it was just too bad, but that didn't mean that you just did nothing. You had to do something. This right now could have been something. And she loved Elizabeth. Elizabeth was her favorite. Even before her disease, she did what she desired: there'd been a lingerie consultant, a personal trainer, trips to Chile and Africa and the Middle East. She pursued. How could you argue with that?

Sarah stood counting her fingers under the warm shield of water.

"Okay, honey," Lauren said. She pulled her from the shower, shut it off. "Get dressed."

"Will you do my hair?"

"We'll see."

But there'd have to be another try; it wasn't the last word. Maybe there never was a last word. She believed in hope. She believed in luck. She believed in mercy, but she didn't know whether mercy meant denial or acceptance.

From the bag she dug out the hair dryer—what a princess, she couldn't help thinking—and began on Sarah. Over the roar her daughter said something, and she couldn't hear it. She clicked off the dryer.

"What?" Lauren said.

"I said thank you," Sarah said.

"Oh," she said, startled. She clicked on the dryer again. "You're welcome."

Sarah had what had been her father's hair, dirty blond, frizzy. Unpredictable. Sarah liked it in pigtails or a braid, to tighten and straighten the wildness. She wanted straight hair. I love your hair, Lauren kept telling her. I don't, she'd say. Every morning and after every shower or bath, she had to have it "straightened." Lauren sprayed it now with a detangler and started hurriedly combing it out. Every time the comb caught, Sarah jumped in pain and Lauren apologized. The other mothers and daughters had already gone. It was just the two of them in the dank locker room. Martin would be standing out in the cold parking lot, Max would be the last howler in the toddler room. Night would have gathered. She kept combing it out and combing it out, but still she could not quite get it straight.

"So how many times are you going to do it?" Martin said, as they slipped into the study and shut the door behind them. He was wearing a set of oven mitts and toting a hockey stick. The room reeked of old cheese.

Lauren stepped up onto a chair. "A few more times, at least."

"What'd the doctor say?" With the stick Martin began to poke around under the baseboard heaters, where he thought the mouse was. For the last day he'd been reasonably sure it was stuck in the study, even if none of the traps had sprung. Maybe the little bastard could live off its fat.

"He said to try it again. There's plenty of stuff."

"Uh-huh."

"You don't really care, do you?"

He pulled back a five-drawer file and tapped on the wood floor. Not a sound. "Of course I do," he said. He got up on the foldout futon sofa and angled the hockey stick over the desk and started poking it deep into blind corners.

"You think it's a dumb idea."

"It was *my* idea. Where the fuck is this guy?"

"Maybe it got out." She started to get down off the chair then stopped herself. "It was *our* idea."

"So try again," he said. He stepped off the sofa and crawled partway under the desk. In the mitts it was hard to grab on to the trunk that contained all their manuscripts, but finally he caught the latch and pulled the trunk back.

"I see something. Pass me the flashlight."

She handed him the flashlight. He pointed it at a brown something that seemed to be oozing out from under the baseboard heater.

"It's either mold or it's our guy." He poked it with the stick. "It's not moving," he said. He pushed and pulled the trunk farther out and lifted up the wires attached to all the computer equipment.

"Is it?"

"Must be."

She handed him the dustpan. With the curved blade of the stick he drew out the little pile. Sometimes, when he'd been chasing it, he thought it might be nine or ten inches long. But now it was curled into a stiffness that could fit into his hand. It was still tentatively connected at the mouth to the pointy needle of the cable wire.

"Ugh," he said.

"Oh," she said. "Look."

It had the coloring of a domestic creature—shades of brown, a streak of white—and a stiffened bushy tail.

"What?"

"It's not a mouse," she said.

"You *said* it was a mouse."

"Well," she said, "it isn't."

He separated its tiny clenched snout from the cable prong and scraped it into the pan, then dumped it into a plastic bag. He took off the oven mitts and knotted the bag, carried it outside to the curb, and carefully stashed it in a can. When he came back in, Lauren was already on her knees washing the corner of the floor.

"We did it," he said.

She looked back at him. "Don't you want me to try again?"

"Of course I want you to try again. Try anything you want."

"You are so full of shit," she said. She crumpled the wet paper towels into a plastic bag and stood and surveyed the study. "None of the wires look chewed into."

"Great," he said.

Holding the bag of fur and crap, she pushed past him toward the study door. "I'm going to try again," she said.

"Of course you are," he said.

For a while, it seemed to her, nobody mentioned it. Richard took his annual two weeks in India and came back and asked not a word about it. Martin called at least twice a week and e-mailed every now and then and said nothing. Sometimes Lauren would call when no one was around, and there was a hitch to her voice—or so it sounded, a kind of forced dullness to it, or a sheen around it—and even Lauren could not bring it up. Of course it had to be left unsaid. When she heard the falseness or the emptiness or the glibness in all of them, she knew not to try to break it. Every morning when she woke, it was Do-Have-Be, Do-Have-Be, making herself go, willing herself not to pack it in.

She looked at her half-packed suitcase. One of them should just tell her. Really it was up to them. It wasn't up to her. She understood. She could just say she understood. They could retreat to that way of talking where you didn't say exactly what you meant, you just said enough around it that people could gather it. That took longer, of course. It wasn't really honest. It disappointed her. Was that the way they would all talk now? When she saw them again would she say, I understand, and would that be the end of it?

"Elizabeth."

He wrapped his thin arms around her. She swore he still smelled of cardamom and curry. *She* wanted to go to India.

He gave her a kiss. "We've got only two hours."

"I know," she said. "I understand." She heard the shift in her voice and turned, but he was already marching from the room to check out timers and alarms. This was ridiculous. He was her husband, for god's sake. It was him. "I understand," she said again, her voice thinner than she wanted it to be but still with an edge to it.

Slowly he came back into the room. He looked at her. He'd heard. What did he think she thought he wanted her to understand? What did you have to accept?

It wasn't over. She wasn't over.

She looked at him slowly, the pale blue eyes, the lightly freckled face, the mouth partly open as if in question, and turned her back and carefully set another piece of clothing into the suitcase.

"What is it?" he said.

"Nothing," she said, her back to him. "I just said I understand, is all. Why don't you check the lamp timer in the guest bedroom."

"All right," he said. She felt him pause in the doorway. "There isn't anything I'm not telling you," he said softly, "if that's what you're thinking."

She glanced at him. He could be like that. He *was* aware. She wanted to hold him. She smiled and shook her head.

"I know," she said.

It was true that sometimes on planes in the last year she'd had to fight the desire for a catastrophic crash. The first plane ride after the bone specialist, it was all she wanted, to go down instantly in a great ball of flame with a whole lot of other people. I don't really want this plane to crash, I just think I do, she wrote, then put her nearly empty notebook away. At least that was brief enough.

"Do you want anything?" Richard asked.

She stretched. "A bigger seat."

"Hah."

"You think it's true that whenever you fly it takes a while for your soul to catch up with you?"

He pried off his shoes. "Maybe."

She sighed. "I guess we could read something."

In their carry-on were the well-thumbed meditations and a few survivor books. He pulled out their checkbook and began ticking through the account. Ever since her retirement she handled all the bills, but he reviewed every expense. Her package had been quite generous, and yet she'd lost four-fifths of her income.

"No trash?" she said.

Grinning, he pulled out a celebrity magazine. "Got it for you right before we boarded."

She leaned her head on his shoulder and began to flip through the pages. Now they both smelled of the inside of the plane. "Thank you," she said.

"I tell you," his mom was saying as they stood in the backyard watching Max wash the playhouse in the wet cold, "this family is falling apart."

"Yup," Martin said.

"Do you exercise at all? How's your drinking?"

"I'm drinking pretty well," he laughed. "My usual two or four a night."

"That's not so good."

"I walk to school."

"I'm afraid you have to do more than that."

He darted over and stopped Max from sponging his hair. "Maybe we ought to go inside," he told him.

"Okay," Max said.

In the kitchen his father snored in a chair while Sarah and Lauren stirred batter for banana bread.

"I want to!" Max shouted.

Martin's father didn't wake.

"He can be like that for hours," Martin's mother said.

"How's he doing anyway?" Martin pulled a chair over for Max and he climbed up, and Lauren handed him a spoon and he reached into the bowl and stirred jerkily.

"He's ruining it!" Sarah said.

"No, he isn't," Lauren said.

"He begins radiation in a month," Martin's mother said.

"Oh," Martin said.

"What's radiation?" Sarah said.

"It's medicine." Lauren swept up the bowl over the children's shouts. "Now we can pour it."

"I want to pour it!" Max shook his spoon at her.

"We all will," she said.

"Is Grandpa sick?" Sarah asked.

"A lot of people are sick," Martin's mother said.

"Help me pour." Lauren slid the baking tin in front of the children and then cautiously offered back the mixing bowl. The three of them held on to it with all hands and she slowly tilted its spout into the tin. The batter oozed out.

"I wish he'd wake up," Martin's mother said.

Lauren handed each of the children a plastic spatula, and they scraped whatever they could into the tin. Max had batter on his chin and both cheeks and near his left eye.

"We're baking bread!" he said.

Lauren took it from the counter and set it in the oven. Max whimpered. "I want bread," he cried.

"It has to bake first."

"I want bread now!" he howled. Lauren picked him up and he kicked, but she still held on to him. "I want my bread!"

"What a cutie," Martin's mother said.

"Can I light the candles?" Sarah whined.

"Not now." Lauren held Max tight so he couldn't kick her. He still howled.

Martin's mother nudged him and pointed to his father. "See, he's still asleep."

He was slumped back in the hard chair, his mouth open, his throat exposed, his stomach out. When Martin was little he used to love poking that big stomach and crawling all over it and bouncing on it.

"You want a glass of wine?" he said.

"Sure," his mother said.

"Lauren?"

"Not yet." Max settled and she stood him on the floor. "You want to go watch TV?"

He wiped at his wet face. "TV." He nodded.

"Me, too?" Sarah said.

"Yes, you, too."

The two of them raced into the living room, and in a few moments Martin could hear the roar of Nickelodeon. He handed his mother a glass of wine. "What do the doctors say?"

She shrugged. "Not much. That it should help. The hormones have helped. They have to put him in some kind of body cast each time he goes for radiation."

"Is he in pain?"

"No more than usual." She took a big sip of wine.

When Martin and his sisters were kids, they used to watch her empty a bottle of Pepsi with one chug. A Mommy sip, they called it. "Do you think I should wake him?"

"How long's he been asleep?"

Lauren looked tiredly at the clock on the microwave. "An hour."

"I want to wake him," Martin's mother said, "but I guess rest isn't bad." She sat in the chair opposite him. "Carl," she said in a low voice, directly to him.

He snored.

"Carl," she said, "it's almost dinnertime."

For an instant his face trembled. His eyes opened. "What?" he yawned.

She shook her head and looked at Lauren. "That's something, isn't it?"

They all laughed.

"When do we eat?" Carl said.

B y   t h e   t i m e she woke, he was gone to morning chants. Muyamaya herself was on the grounds, and Elizabeth felt a twinge of excitement. Muyamaya knew about her, had even given her a scarf. They were humbled by her attention and did not confide about it to anyone.

She got up stiffly and opened the curtain. They were miles outside of Bridgetown, in an area that looked like a landing strip. She took a long bath and forced herself to dress. She sat on the bed and dug out her first bag of vits. It took her twenty minutes to take them all.

Downstairs she wandered the lobby. Every foursome of leather chairs was occupied by people sipping tea or a frothy pink punch. She bought a package of rice cakes and munched them as she leaned against a wall. They were dry. She bought a bottle of water and sipped it slowly until it was finished.

She couldn't quite shake the slowness and the pain. If she attended any of the sessions, she knew she'd fall instantly asleep, although that would be explained away as a higher level of meditation. She didn't want to fall asleep in a chair. At the concierge desk she scheduled an afternoon massage.

"You know that's during the plenary session," he said.

She nodded. She didn't care.

Unwilling to return to the room, she finally found an empty leather chair. It was like sitting on a dead cow. She dozed.

"Elizabeth?"

She forced her eyes open. It was . . .

"Mark," he said for her. "How are you?"

She looked at him. She couldn't remember how they knew each other or if he knew about her problem. Though almost everyone knew.

"I'm a little exhausted," she said.

"Obviously. But how *are* you?" He looked her in the eyes to see if he could tell.

She shrugged.

"Well." He smiled. "I've got to get to the next session. You coming?"

She shook her head. "I'd like to."

"You're not going to hear Richard?"

She knew what an honor it was that he was getting to lead a chant. "Another time," she said.

"Another time." He hurried off.

Even here, even now, it was like running a race where she couldn't keep up, or like she was the only one running and all the others stood on the side, empathetic, voyeuristic, waiting for her to be over.

She tried to linger outside the auditorium for Richard's chant, but the crowd spilled over and she couldn't even see inside. She surrendered to her room for a nap. For some reason her other shoulder hurt. She tried to massage it away, a gnawing heat around the blade. The bed was horrid.

Later, on the table in a towel while the woman worked on her, she kept waiting for the pain to change. It was still there. Right there. Goddamn. In the room, when Richard returned, his face all bright with success, and asked how she was, she couldn't bring herself to tell him. "Fine," she said. Whenever he wasn't looking she swung her shoulder around and around. She sent him off to dinner by himself.

Though he wouldn't be alone, she knew. He had so many admirers. He'd been with the ashram over twenty years, but recently, they said, he was *emerging*. He told everyone it was the Epiphany courses he'd begun taking, and now other people from the ashram were signing up. Three hours a night, three times a week. He was really growing and she admired that, but he'd begun the course work because he needed to be stronger for her, and now it was taking him farther away. He promised this would be his last session.

When he came up after evening chants, he was exhausted and exhilarated. He tried to tell her all about what he'd eaten at dinner and with whom, as if she cared through the searing in her shoulder.

"What's the matter?" he said.

"Just tired."

Instantly he slept. When she looked at him this way, in the slackness against the pillow, in all that restfulness that he so easily entered, she couldn't help thinking that he was saving himself for his next wife.

When his parents had left and they had their house back to themselves, she sat on the couch with a glass of wine and the newspaper and tried not to think about anything. She read the Sunday engagement section and magazine, raked in the faces of all those up-and-coming couples and perfect women. Martin sat with his back to her, holding a four-finger scotch and flipping from one sports channel to the next. They hadn't fooled around in seven weeks. It felt like one long endless slide, as if they'd rolled the wrong number and found themselves tumbling down into a place so far behind that it wasn't a question of catching up anymore, they were just trying to stay on the board. She took a gulp of wine and rifled through for the Week in Review.

"I've been thinking," Martin said, turning from his chair.

She rose with the rest of her wine and a last section of the paper. "Just don't make any calls tonight, okay?"

He sat watching the repeating highlights, the television glazing his knees. One more drink couldn't hurt, if he could just up and go get it.

When he woke it was past three and the guys on the screen were still talking about tonight and tomorrow as the station looped them around with the highlights. If he waited for another few minutes he could say the one-liners along with them. He felt sober, not hungover. He poured himself a seltzer and dialed her number.

"What are you doing up?" she said.

"The usual." He looked around in the dark kitchen for something to distract himself with. "How are you feeling?"

"Fine. I'm fine."

"How was Bridgetown?"

"Good."

It was indifference; she just couldn't bring herself to say anything else.

"Well, I . . ." He opened the microwave door and inspected the crusted stains on the glass tray. Pizza. Mashed potato. Milk. "I don't know whether this thing is going to happen."

"Of course it isn't going to happen," she said.

"I didn't say that."

"It's all right, really. You know I'm not in a place where I can handle anything beyond me. Richard's not around much."

His head hurt. "I was thinking we all might come over there for the summer."

"I don't need any sympathy visits," she said. "I don't need anybody feeling obligated."

"It'd be fun," he said.

"Maybe."

"Well, you think about it."

"*You* think about it."

"So what else is going on?"

"Nothing is going on. Whatever gave you the idea that anything is going on?"

"How's Richard?"

"He gets in at midnight, then he wants to talk, then he falls asleep. Then I'm all awake." She took a breath. "I get wound up."

"Hmm." He shut the microwave door. "I guess I should get to bed."

"All right. Thanks for calling."

"Love you."

"Love you."

"So how are we going to do this?" Lauren said. "I mean, I know we *can* do it, but how are we going to do it?"

"We're just going to," Martin said.

"Is cancer contagious?" Sarah asked.

Martin looked at her. "Where'd you get that idea?"

"You know, can you catch it?"

"*No.*"

"I think I'd rather stay with Grace this summer."

"You *love* Aunt Elizabeth."

"I don't wanna be away for the whole summer," she said tearfully. "I won't have any friends."

"Max will be there. We'll be there. Aunt Elizabeth and Uncle Richard will be there."

"It's not the same."

"I know, sweetie. I know. But you always have fun when we go away."

"You can't keep doing this to me," she cried. "And now I don't even get to pick the place!" She ran upstairs and slammed herself into her room.

"So, you just said it was all right? You didn't think of asking me or anything?"

"Maybe they won't come," she said tiredly.

"I want them to come. I just wish you'd asked me."

"Can they come?" she asked.

"Of course they can come." He looked around at the perfect house. "How long do you think they're going to stay?"

"Ten or twelve weeks."

"Good god."

"We'll paint after they leave."

"Two little kids—we're certainly not going to do any touching up beforehand."

"I never said we were."

He pulled out his electronic calendar, punched in access numbers. "I might need to be away for a part of that time." He typed with his index finger. "Maybe half of it."

"I could tell them to rent an apartment."

"That's all right." He closed his calendar and smiled. "They don't have any money anyway."

"I need you, too," she said.

"Maybe you're just being needy."

He shut himself in the meditation room, saw Muyamaya, took a cleansing breath. Oh that was wrong, that was wrong. But what else could he say when the only mantra that ever came to him these days was *I am absent, I am absent.* People had no idea—*no idea*—what his life was like, what their life was like. They'd been in their prime, he'd loved his job, she'd made a lot of money, and they'd take on anything. She was fearless. She wanted it all and she tried *everything*. Once they'd gotten lost in the snow in the Italian Alps—a storm had come up so late in the season it was practically an illusion—and they'd stepped into a miracle of a trekkers' hut and sat up all night sipping scotch and even—even made love when they were supposed to be worried for their lives. The next day they'd walked out. Now they had to try everything just to survive, and they had to live with it and figure out how to live beyond it at the same time. Practically every week a new therapist came to the house, or she bought a new remedy or she took a trip somewhere to work with somebody. She had to devote herself to it, and he tried to devote himself to her. And now she was going to draw a line around the summer and have them both give in to it. He supposed he could go off to Bridgetown, maybe do an Epiphany course in Amsterdam, and see where the firm might send him. Twelve weeks wasn't so long. Just a whole bloody summer. But what was she thinking? Was this another one of those moments when you got caught in the middle and you just had to wait your way out?

What about *them*? He opened the door and looked over the stairs. She was standing under the crystals in the foyer. He padded down to her.

"I'm sorry," he said. "I just get a little tense, that's all."

"You like your space," she said.

"I do."

"I'm not saying I'm dying," she said. "I'm just saying time is precious, and I want to be with them and I want to be with you."

"Okay," he said.

She sniffled. "You think I'm being a shit, don't you?"

"Darling. Sweets." He touched her cheek, held her. "You need to do what you have to. Me, too. Right?"

"Right," she said.

"I'm sorry about the other thing."

"No, you're not."

"Then I'm sorry about not being sorry. I'm going back upstairs. Okay?"

She nodded. "Okay."

FURTHER
QUESTIONS

I have to apologize for calling you at home like this," the provost was saying in that measured voice of his, "and so early at that. But I'm afraid I had no choice. Jane Wilson . . . ah . . . it seems that one of our students, Jane Wilson, hung herself late last night."

"Jane Wilson?" Martin said, sitting up in bed in the still-dark room. That wasn't Jane Doyle. Who was she?

"I'm afraid so," the provost said. "We're all terribly saddened about this. Can you make a noon meeting in my office?"

"Of course."

"See you then."

Jane Wilson? She was in his residential seminar on living anthropology. He could not quite summon her. Indifferent brown hair, combed back. Her face puffy and sallow. She'd just handed in a paper on Friday.

"Jane Wilson?" Lauren whispered beside him.

"A student," he said. "Suicide."

"Oh no."

On his walk to the class, Martin avoided knots of students talking in hushed or loud voices, excited, gossipy, stricken. The dorm was locked. He looked around for a phone or a doorbell. He pounded on the door.

No answer.

All the students had dispersed to their classes. He pounded on the dorm door again. Nothing. The class was held in the basement. He hiked around to where he thought the window was and bent down. They were there in the cramped room. He knocked. They were all talking. He knocked again.

"The professor," someone called out.

"Could you let me in?" he shouted through the closed window while pointing toward the side door.

Geoff opened the door for him. He was tall and pale, with red hair falling across his face as if he'd just woken up. Martin hated teaching in the dorms.

"I got locked out," he said.

"We had to." Geoff hurried ahead of him down the stairs, toward the class. "There were too many people coming through."

"I understand."

In the room the students looked at him, expectant, tinged with misery. "I guess you heard what happened," he said. They nodded. "We're not going to have class today." They nodded again. "But we can talk about it, if you want. Or you can leave."

No one left. A sorrow for all of them leaped from his

heart—even for the lacrosse player who was always late and hadn't turned anything in yet, and for the stoner who made too many sarcastic remarks—and he fought to restrain it. He sat cross-legged on his desk and waited.

"She killed herself," a girl said. "I just saw her Friday."

"I saw her yesterday afternoon," a guy who had taken out a pack of cigarettes said.

"And?" the girl said.

"Nothing. I just saw her."

"Does it make any of you feel like killing yourselves?" That was—thank god—not Martin who asked. It was one of the students. There were nods and groans.

"I tried once," someone whispered. He could barely catch who it was.

"I haven't thought about it since I was a freshman," a junior said.

And he sat there, for the hour, letting them run their encounter session. He said as little as possible. At the end there was a kind of sigh, and they all looked at him, deflated. He had to say something. His face grew hot and he knew he was blushing, and he'd long since ceased to blush in front of students and this made him hotter and redder.

"You just—we just—need to be as kind to one another as we can," he said. "Because we can never know if it will be the last time we have." Kindness, he was teaching them kindness. The faculty handbook said to teach Truth and Art. There was some truth in kindness—perhaps some art, too—but did he have to sound like a goddamn Hallmark card?

As he walked to his office, he jammed his hands deeper into his pockets and tersely shook his head. Nailed to the brick wall of the dining hall were banners. WE MISS YOU. GOD BLESS YOU! A few wrapped bouquets sagged on the lawn. Along the path toward him marched Annka. He swallowed a gasp. Now, as he looked at her, he tried to feel a complexity in her face that would speak to him, that would tell him she was capable of empathy. She taught less than he did and she made nearly twice as much money, and all he could see behind the clear-framed glasses, framed by the blond hair pulled back into a bun, was that she was capable of empathizing with herself.

"Hello, Martin." She smiled quietly. "How are you holding up?"

"Fine, I think. And you?"

"You know." Again she smiled without teeth, her pointy chin pointed down. "It's hard."

"Did you have her in any classes?" he asked gently.

"Oh no," she said, as if, had the girl been under her instruction, she would never have killed herself.

"She was in mine."

"I know." Her hand fluttered at her side. He was relieved it did not touch him. Briefly they waited for the clock tower to toll. It didn't.

"I just had the class she was in," he said anyway.

"I know." Now she patted him on the shoulder. He recoiled. She looked at him, still tightly smiling. "We missed you at the town meeting this morning. It was *so* cathartic." Again her chin dipped toward the ground. "I sang a solo of a hymn."

This time the clock did toll. He could have kissed it. "I have to run," he said.

"There were more than a thousand people there," she called after him. "It was *really* something."

He hurried back to his building. She sang hymns? In his office the voice mail light blinked its orange bulb. He dialed Lauren.

"Hey," he said.

"I know," she said, "we missed the town meeting. But listen, Elizabeth called. She thinks Richard has left."

"What?" he said. At the mention of her name, he'd been all prepared for awful medical news. This was somehow . . . worse? Better?

"I could tell you more, but she's waiting for your call."

"Uh-huh." He felt his stomach beginning to cave. The last time he'd seen Jane Wilson, she'd smiled shyly as she passed in her paper.

"Too bad we couldn't make that baby happen," Lauren said.

S h e ' d   c o m e back from what . . . what. Shopping? The spa? Someplace neutral. Someplace she couldn't quite name. And there was something not subtle about the house. Something off. He wasn't due for another few hours, but she sensed a dysfunction beyond the usual dysfunction. An opening, a hole, a gap, a chasm. Her mother had tried to warn her. Missing. He had gone.

Three pairs of shoes missing from the closet, two sweaters from the drawer, and, when she brought out the ladder and climbed to the attic door and pushed it open, a carry-on from the attic. Had he told her he was going? In the kitchen she checked the calendar. Against her cheek she felt for the impression of his last kiss. There wasn't one. She called his office. His voice mail. "I can't come to the phone right now, but if you leave a message, I'll get back to you." He didn't have a secretary or an assistant. She called the main number.

"Richard Perkins," she said.

"I'll put you through—"

"I just—"

And there he was again. "I can't come to the phone right now . . ."

She hung up. Was there a note in some secret place? Her pillow? The bath? On top of the goddamn telly? In the refrigerator? Inside the microwave? The checkbook? He'd left the checkbook, not a check missing. He had credit cards, a bank card.

"Richard," she called.

The phone rang. She snatched it up.

"Hello?" she said.

"Is this Elizabeth Kreutzel-Perkins?"

"Yes."

"I'm afraid I have a message for you."

"Go on."

"Your ball therapy session for Thursday has been canceled. Alan has taken ill."

Good Christ. "Thank you," she said.

"We will reschedule." Reshedwell. Brits.

She hung up the phone.

"Richard," she said uncertainly, as if just saying the name might break the plumbing.

That was all hours ago. She'd combed out her hair, stuck on a morphine patch, decided which rings to leave which nieces, and then had a glass of wine and a chat with Lauren across the pond. She wasn't quite ready for her mother. The wine felt awful in her stomach, at the back of her throat, along the crust of her brain, wherever it went. The morphine tried very hard to take the edge off, but seemed only to make everything more jagged. Uncomfortable. Tangled. In a disarray.

Ray, ray, ray, the house seemed to say.

The phone.

"Hello," she slurred.

"Elizabeth?"

"Hey. Thanks for getting back to me so quickly." It was good to hear his American voice. It was good to hear her own American going back to him.

"Are you sure about this?"

"Yes."

"I can get there on Friday."

"That would be great," she said.

"Anything else?"

"I hope not."

"Well, we have a little crisis here. I've got to—"

"Really?" She tried to feel interested. "What?"

"One of my students." His voice dropped to something

almost below a whisper. "Killed herself," he said. "Anyway, I've got to go. Love you."

"Love you."

She hung up and stared at the blank television. There'd be hours and hours for it. She could see herself hooking up to it like it was another dose of pamidronate. All these people who lay solitarily—was that a word?—dying in their hospital beds, gazing at a last football game or talk show. She already knew that she was alone. Was this going to be such a big deal? So he was gone. So she was alone alone. She'd be alone in her coffin, for god's sake.

Maybe he was her cancer. Maybe he had his own cancer. Maybe they could squeeze into that box together.

She switched on the telly.

"Do you know," asked the girl's biology professor, "if there's anything like client privilege between us and her?"

The provost shrugged. On the surface he was always affable, almost dopey. You could fall asleep to his lush, modulated voice. "I don't think, and I'm not going to suggest, that we need to be adversarial." He smiled at the five professors around the table. "If you know anything, you need to be honest about it. But for the sake of privacy, we all"—and here he nodded at two attorneys to his right—"feel that no one *needs* to speak to the press. For the family's sake, the less public speculation—or even analysis—the better." He frowned slightly and then relaxed his face in a gesture of neutrality and harmlessness. "We'll work with the authorities. We'll work with all parties. But we have no official stake in this. We're not asking to be in any loop. Every loss of this nature"—now he was quoting an e-mail he'd sent that morning—"is both private and communal. It is with us all. Further questions?"

"I told you I could see this coming," Martin's mom said. "Didn't I?"

"Yes." He tried to hide his impatience. "Yes, you had an inkling."

"An inkling." She bit into what sounded like an apple. "Let me tell you, we've known a lot of people who've had this kind of thing, and none of them, and I mean *none of them,* have devoted themselves to it the full-time way that she has."

"And what happened to them?" he had to ask.

"They died."

"Well, maybe that's just it. Maybe you have to do it full-time to have a chance to live."

"I don't think so." She took another bite. "I think he probably had another—you know—woman."

"So you've said." Martin thought of hanging up, but she was one person you couldn't hang up on.

"Or he's gay. Or bi. Or whatever you call it."

"Whatever," Martin said.

"Good thing Lauren isn't having that baby."

"Mom."

"So when do you leave?"

He told her. Then, to get her off his sister, he told her about his student.

"Did you know her?"

He tried to give her as much as he could stand, and she riddled him with questions about what she was like.

"What do you have to do with any investigation?" she asked.

"I don't really know."

"Well." She finished her apple. "If you need any help, you can always call Martha."

"Mom." He swallowed whatever he could think of saying. "I've got to go."

"Call from Elizabeth's."

"I will."

He set the phone on the charger and stared at the suitcase he'd been trying to pack while he'd talked to her. He'd forgotten underwear. Max toddled in and stuck to his knees.

"I'll miss you," the boy said.

"I'll miss you, too."

He took up his son and felt him sinking into him, the chest against his shoulder, the head heavy and dropping into his neck, the warm breath on the hollow of skin around his collarbone. Max rested there. Then he pushed himself up and pointed.

"TV?" he said.

"Okay," Martin said. He picked up the remote and clicked it on, and Max wriggled free and sat on top of the suitcase, watching. The phone rang. He let it go. From downstairs, he heard Lauren pick up. He tried to listen closely. It was someone she didn't know that well. She called to him to get on.

"Hello?" he said.

124

"Professor Kreutzel?"

Somebody official. God, he hadn't even helped out with the laundry or dinner or the kids or whatever else was down there in the toy-strewn swirl of the kitchen and dining room and living room. He wanted to say no, he was just another numb nut watching an almost-three-year-old watch TV, while his skull closed itself tighter and tighter over his brain and his lids clenched over his eyes and his dick shriveled into minisculity and his balls withered and shrank—

"What," he said. "What is it?"

In the emptiness she heard the ruffle and smack of the morning mail being pushed through the door slot. A dull gray light spread across the ceiling and out into the hall. At her elbow, at the base of her neck, and at the top of her skull various niggles announced themselves. Hot spots, one of the healers had called them. And she understood him to mean that these were zones where tumors could erupt at any moment.

She plunked her way downstairs and cut and ground wheatgrass and then drank it from last night's wineglass as if she were trying to turn her stomach out. She sat at the table and began taking her vits. The doorbell rang its lame, cranky ring, and she rose to answer it.

"Martin!" For some reason she'd thought it was tomorrow he was coming.

"Elizabeth," he said.

They hugged.

"I thought it was tomorrow," she said.

He set his bag in the foyer and followed her into the kitchen with his briefcase.

"Do you want something to drink?"

"Wine," he said hoarsely. "Or scotch."

She smiled and pulled out an unopened bottle of thirty-year-old scotch.

"You shouldn't," he said.

"Richard's." She shook her head.

"Oh, well then." He took it from her and tore it open. He grabbed what little ice there was in the pocket-sized freezer and poured a few fingers. He took a sip. "Wow," he said.

"Can I smell it?"

He held it to her nose. It was smoky, peaty—whatever—but she bet it was smooth anyway. She pushed it back to him.

"So what's the plan?"

She looked at him and tried to tell how scared he was for her. "I have reiki at eleven," she said. "Other than that . . ." She shrugged her shoulders.

"What do you want to do?"

"*Want* to do?" She felt the tears start and strangled them back. There were so many choices! "I don't have anything I *want* to do," she said.

He reached for his briefcase. "I brought you some magazines." He stopped himself. "I don't mean to be this pathetic."

"Neither do I."

They stood looking at each other.

"Shit," she said.

"I guess." He looked at the ceiling, then made himself look back at her. "I guess it must have felt to him like I was acting like he wasn't here."

"Maybe," she said. "Maybe. But there was a lot of time he was acting like *I* wasn't here."

"You don't want to find him?"

"I don't know." She continued inspecting the floor. "Sometimes I think he'll come back when he's ready, and sometimes I know this is it. You know. The beginning of my end."

"God," he said.

"It's not so bad. I mean, it's awful. But if you take away reasons for living—or if they go away all by themselves—then this whole thing makes sense."

"So you're just going to lay down and die?" He took a big swallow of scotch.

She forced a laugh. "Some people do. When they're ready. And some people fight and they still die. And some people fight and they get to live. Maybe he knows I'm not going to get to live—"

"And maybe he's just a selfish asshole."

"A lot of people think I'm the selfish one."

"Everyone's selfish," he tried.

"When you're in a lot of pain," she said, "you sink more and more into yourself. Nobody can jump in to join you."

"This is cheerful," he said.

"You're the only one I can say this to." She wiped her eyes. "You won't lose it."

127

"I just drink." He shook the ice in the otherwise empty glass. She watched as he poured himself another. "I bet he's at one of the ashrams."

"I don't need to know." She pointed at his briefcase. "Are you going to hand over those magazines or what?"

When he woke she was pulling up the window dressings to sunlight and trying to smile at him.

"It's one o'clock," she said. "You want to go for lunch?"

He remembered. "Your reiki?"

"It was good."

He wasn't hungover, just fuzzy with jet lag. "Lunch?" he mumbled.

"It's sunny," she said. "It's never sunny here."

He pulled on shoes and followed her downstairs. He looked at the calendar hanging on the side of the refrigerator.

"It's March," he told himself.

"You ready?"

He splashed water on his face and tried to feel clear.

She drove with the top down, in and out of roundabouts, across a bridge, through a truck barricade, from one high street to the next. He had no idea where they were, but the neighborhoods kept seeming neater and trendier. Every time they stopped at a light she kneaded her shoulder.

"Maybe it's just a muscle or a joint thing," she said.

"Have you told Sparks?"

She looked at him. "My scans aren't supposed to be for another month."

"Hmm." He took in the wind. "You should probably tell her. Does Richard know?"

"No."

After forty or fifty minutes, they were where she wanted them to be. She slammed out of the car and bought a parking stub and stuck it in the windshield, and he helped her close the top.

"That's the longest I've driven in months," she said. Her face was gray and yellow, and she looked brittle. "I hope it's worth it."

They walked down streets lined with sweater boutiques and shoe stores and French-looking cafés. He'd forgotten London could be this nice. His eyes seemed foggy and he kept rubbing them.

"You'll wake up," she said. "It just takes a while."

They sat in a restaurant with blond wood floors and Scandinavian chairs. The menu seemed Californian. He ordered a glass of wine.

"If I'm going to feel this blurry . . . ," he explained.

She pointed to where her morphine patch usually was, a dulled square of skin. "That's how I always feel."

"It's not on," he said. "That's good."

"The reiki. And you're here. I don't usually slip it on and off like this, but it's time to try something new."

He ate salmon while she nibbled a special plate of lentils, *haricots verts*, carrots, and romaine. "Richard was always saying I should live a little," she said. "Maybe he was just trying to kill me off."

He laughed. It was a joke, wasn't it?

"I like this place."

"Your salmon," she said. "Can I try?"

He nodded and began sliding her his plate. She forked off a piece and ate it.

"That's really good," she said.

"Uh-huh." A guy at Sloan-Kettering had told them that the most important thing was for her to keep her weight up. "You want some more?"

"Nope."

Afterward they window-shopped. He kept missing Lauren. At an undergarment store an older woman listened to Elizabeth and looked her over. "So madam doesn't want a string?" she said incredulously. "Madam wants a proper pair of panties?" Then Elizabeth led him into a sweater shop and began trying on pullovers in purples, reds, and oranges. She found one she liked.

"I'll buy it for you," he offered.

"You don't have to."

"I *want* to."

It was almost two hundred pounds! He practically choked when he paid.

"Thank you," she said. And kissed him on the cheek.

He should offer to drive them home, but he had never driven in London.

"It's all right," she insisted. "I can do it. And it will be faster on the way back."

He sat in the passenger seat, appalled by how much he'd spent—the cab in from Heathrow, the lunch, the sweater. The plane ticket.

The traffic dripped from the city. She kept rubbing her shoulder.

"Come on," she said. "Come on."

"Pull over," he said.

"You sure?"

"Absolutely."

It took a few more minutes—all of half a block—until there was curb space, something that resembled a fire hydrant. They got out and exchanged seats.

"It'll be easier in a little car," he said.

"I wish the seats went back."

She closed her eyes behind the sunglasses, and he shifted the car into gear. Almost instantly someone let him into the flow.

"This isn't going to be so bad."

"Keep straight for a couple of lights. Then at the next roundabout take Marble Arch."

"You can nap in between," he tried to cheer her.

"I hope so." Her eyes, he could tell, were still shut. She wanted to move her shoulder around, but there was no space in the Alfa Romeo.

"Scream if you want."

"I'm going to," she said.

It was easy, in such slow traffic. He could practically shut his eyes. Then the roundabout came.

"Keep to the left," she said.

"Keep to the left," he muttered. "Keep to the left."

The sign for Marble Arch came up, and he turned onto it easily. To the left. To the left.

"Four or five lights," she said. "Then Dunkers Green at the roundabout."

The road widened to two lanes his way. He stayed to the left, although the traffic moved as if it were still the fast lane. But right was passing, wasn't it? He glanced at her. She appeared to be asleep. He stayed left. Cars kept trying to cut over, and he kept letting them in. At least he'd had only a glass to drink, and that was hours ago. He was definitely sober.

So they were together but they were apart. He had a spouse and children, she had neither. He was for the moment—and as far as he knew—well, and she was living under her sentence. He had a job, she had her retirement. They were as separate as when she was nine and he five, and she could have and do all the things that he wanted but couldn't, because she was old enough. He used to lie sobbing in his bed at eight o'clock on a summer evening, listening to them all playing Wiffle ball in the driveway, the sky filled with daylight. Or when they went out to a restaurant with booths, Martha and Elizabeth took one to themselves while he was stuck in the other with his parents. He'd felt endlessly shut off from everything then, and it seemed to him that just when he gained a new level of independence, of freedom, his sisters had gone on to an even higher level, and as the youngest, he appeared to be more ornamental than essential, the object to be coddled and shackled and, whenever his mother's punishments began, protected and resented.

She was lying in her bed, her eyes shut, the morphine patch reattached, talking about her scars, while he sat on a wooden chair and tried to listen, even though he had heard it all before. *Dis-ease* meant that there was something inside that had come from outside that had triggered the illness, and Elizabeth believed this something to have first come from their mother, from the humiliations and slappings and beltings she inflicted, and then later from the work Elizabeth had chosen, which in part was a result of the way their mother had treated her. She believed that if she had grown up in a more open and loving home, she would have turned to a life more open and loving than the straitjacket of IPOs and mergers and deals that she'd eagerly strapped herself into. Both Martha and Elizabeth always said that his life was the freest because he'd had the most freedom growing up, but he didn't recall it that way, and he couldn't see it that way now either. He earned much less than they did, and couldn't afford the freedom he thought his sisters had. Perhaps none of them were free. Only really rich, really healthy people were free. Whenever he met any of those, he hated them.

Rage was a cheap fuel, but whenever he was with her after her diagnosis he shut it up inside, and so he had been even less honest and less human with her than he was with himself. There were times that he doubted he was even a person anymore, and he saw he had assumed a role that he thought the situation required, and in that way, then, they'd really switched places. He'd put on the straitjacket that her dis-ease had forced her to rip off.

". . . and that time," she was saying, "when I dropped that vase."

He nodded his head, still unable to recall it, but

perfectly capable of remembering how she recalled it, after all the times she'd told it. A party when she was six or seven, the house filled with friends of their parents. She'd picked up a vase from an end table and for one reason or another carried it toward another end table, only to have the vase slip from her hands and shatter against the floor. Their mom had swooped in, whisked down Elizabeth's pants and underwear, right there in front of twenty or thirty people, and spanked her bare bottom.

"Yes," he said, "I know."

But he wanted to say: Get over it. Does it always have to be about this?

"I'm so tired," she said.

"Could you sleep?"

"I don't know. Can you sit there?"

"Sure."

He watched her try to sleep, her head stiffly straight and square on the pillow, her neck exposed, her short hair fallen to the side, her sallow cheeks slightly indenting, her eyes tightly shut, as she made herself breathe slowly, deeper. The last of the gray light fell from the window, and darkness began to arrive in a tightening of the walls against bleakness, in the despair that could come at the end of the day, of the things that still had to be done, of things that would have to be left undone. Any joy at evening—at having gotten through the rush of the day's business—was rarely something he could feel without a drink, or two or three or four. They still had dinner to decide on and gather and eat and dishes to wash and the first part of the night to get through, and then a second, later, more endless part when she would try to sleep but she couldn't, and he'd be the only one here, and because she would have slept in this early, early part the later part would be that much worse and he'd have to be of use. But now she slept.

He shifted soundlessly on his chair, looked around for something to read or do, set his feet up on the unoccupied side of the bed. He'd been to Hamburg with her to see a jolly doctor who twiddled his thumbs and promised to make her a "cookbook" of treatment plans, but never did. He'd been to some of the worst of the appointments in Hampstead, when Richard said he couldn't go, and afterward he'd sat with her in the oncology suite while she took in three hours of IV pamidronate and asked him to dial around to give the latest news of her situation. Once, when he persuaded her to come to Sloan-Kettering for just one more second opinion (a third opinion, a fourth opinion), they'd stood side by side in the overcrowded waiting room while a row of people resituated themselves so he and she could sit together. "Everyone is so polite," he'd said. "Yeah," she'd murmured, "like Auschwitz." To which there were a hundred things he could have said, but didn't.

"Has he called you?" Martin's mother wanted to know.

"No," Lauren said tiredly.

"Well, I haven't heard a word. But I'm almost afraid to call."

She nodded her head, even though his mother

couldn't see her. The water for the pasta was boiling, and she stuck in half a box's worth of linguine.

"So, how're you doing? Do you want us to come out there?"

"We're fine," she said gaily. She could just picture all the cleaning she'd have to do to make the house presentable.

"And you're teaching all his classes, too? That's unbelievable."

"Uh-huh." She stirred a little olive oil into the cooking pasta.

"I guess it's too late to call anyway."

"It's pretty late."

"Didn't he say he'd call?"

"Well, you know how it is."

"Can you talk to Carl for a minute?"

"Sure." She stirred the pasta once more.

"How's my daughter-in-law?" Carl said, his voice chalky.

"Good," she said. "How are *you*?"

"Can't complain. Can't complain."

She liked him and she felt empathy for him, but she just didn't have the time. "Well," she said.

"Did you see the paper today?" He'd somehow arranged for them to receive the *Wall Street Journal* for free.

"Not yet," she said.

"There's an article in there you might find useful."

"Oh?"

"I'll clip it and send it to you."

"I can find it," she said.

"Really, it's no bother." He let out a hacking cough.

"What page?"

"One of the front pages. The one about Internet teaching."

"I'll find it," she insisted.

"Good. How's the weather there?"

God, she could just scream. The sink still had breakfast dishes, and she didn't want to think what Sarah's book bag still had in it. It hadn't been unpacked. "Cold," she said.

"Same here. Although it got sunny for a little while. Did you have that?"

"I can't remember," she said.

"I see."

"I'm sorry. I've got to go."

"Okay."

"I'll call as soon as I hear—"

"Wait a minute. She wants the last word."

"You'll call us?" She was on the line that quickly. "Or we'll call you."

"Right," Lauren said.

"You sound pretty busy. You sure you don't want us to come out there?"

"Positive."

"Well, let us know if you change your mind."

"I will, I will."

"Can you say good-bye to him?"

Aargh! "I—"

"Thanks for taking the time," Carl said.

"Anytime," she said. "Talk to you soon."

"Good-bye."

She clicked off the phone and glared at it. They were nice people. She loved them, but—

"Dinner in ten minutes," she shouted into the living room.

Again the phone rang. She could never figure out how to turn the ringer off—they'd lost the instructions as soon as they'd opened the box. She turned her back to the ringing and stirred the pasta. Finally it stopped, but the machine didn't pick up. Max had.

"Max!" she said. "We're going to eat soon."

He chatted away as if he couldn't hear her. He was talking about TV and Daddy being in London and today was fine and he was great. Then he strayed over to her and handed her the phone.

"Hello?" she said.

"Hey, sweetie, just thought I'd check in."

Her mother. She gripped the big spoon as if she might thrash it against the stove top. Why couldn't she ever tell these people that now wasn't a good time? "Hi," she said. "How are you?"

"Martin?"

He heard it, but he was in the dark, his feet up, descending, they hadn't landed yet, he didn't need to quite wake yet, and then customs and the guy with the hired car, and the long, clogged ride into Dunkers Green and missing Jane Wilson's funeral. He didn't have to open his eyes quite yet.

"Martin?"

He moved his feet, felt his shoulders swell into the chair back, still landing. No, they weren't moving. They'd landed.

"Are we here?" he said.

"We slept a long time."

"Oh."

"I haven't slept that long in ages."

"Uh-huh." There was a dim lamp lit on the bedside table. She was standing, stretching herself out, wincing, looking at him. "What time is it?"

"Two."

"*Two?*" He looked at his feet stretched out on the bed. "I slept in a chair."

"You probably thought you were still on the plane."

"I did. I did." He wasn't even sure he could move.

"Are you hungry?"

"I don't know."

"You must be. Come on."

He unfolded himself from the chair, and she turned on lights as she made her way downstairs. Two o'clock. Nine there—post-bedtime. He ought to wait another hour. He and Elizabeth would probably be up all night anyway.

He had one of Richard's beers and tried to help, but he didn't know the kitchen and he kept bumping into her as he banged around the drawers and cabinets looking for the right pan, the right packet of rice. Finally they sat at the table while the meal cooked on the stove top. He was almost awake.

"I think he's got a little hash somewhere, if you like," she said.

"I'm all right."

"It's probably where he went . . ."

"Amsterdam?" Now he was awake.

"Oh yeah." She smiled. "Saunas. Coffee bars."

"Sounds like he'd be easy to find."

"You're just looking for an excuse," she teased him.

He drained his beer and got up and headed toward the fridge. "Just another way I could wreck things," he said.

"It wasn't you."

"It's never anybody." He found the last beer and brought it back to the table.

"The weird thing is I thought we were getting so much better. He was *a lot better*." She glanced around the kitchen. "He cooked. He cleaned. He was much more present."

She couldn't look back at Martin.

"Oh shit," she said.

He was over pretty quickly, he thought, holding her, hugging her. She gasped as she cried. She hadn't ever cried that much with him, he thought. He had an essential coldness that somehow made her keep it together. Maybe he was at heart just cold. Maybe that's why Jane Wilson had never come to talk with him.

"Easy," he said. "Easy."

"I could find him," he said.

"Please don't."

But in her tumble she couldn't tell whether he heard her, or even whether she meant it.

"I mean it," she said. She reached for something, and

he saw it was the Kleenex and he tore one out and handed it to her.

"I'm tougher than this," she said.

"I know."

The food got cooked and they ate. She was silent and sober. He knew if it were him and not her, he'd probably be getting stoned all the time—or at least a lot—just to get himself out of his body and out of his mind and out of the world, to find the sensation of just what that meant. Too bad there wasn't another beer in the fridge. He'd love to get stoned. But if she didn't, he shouldn't. He was thirty-eight, for god's sake. But maybe he was just slowly killing himself. Maybe the next time Dowler drilled up his asshole he'd find what they were all waiting for. Maybe it was already there, and getting stoned or not getting stoned didn't matter. Maybe in his stomach. Or, like his dead uncle whom he never knew, in his brain. Sometimes he wanted to live and sometimes he just wanted to die. There was a lot of pleasure in life, but once you were really sick you couldn't find it anymore.

"What are you thinking about?" she asked.

"Nothing."

He stumbled up and cleared the table. At the sink he washed the dishes. She was gone. Probably into that little room to meditate. Or in the living room doing her chigong. He spied into the living room. She was there, in an old pink T-shirt and baggy green sweats, standing, moving as if underwater, doing stuff. That was a good sign. They ought to go out and find her a nice sweat suit.

Good stuff might make her feel better. Maybe their next outing she'd wear the sweater he'd bought. Maybe—

The door was rattling as if someone was sticking a key in it. He stared at it. Wasn't it three or four o'clock?

"Elizabeth," he whispered.

She was still chi-gonging, unable or unwilling to hear him.

"Elizabeth!"

Reluctantly she came out into the foyer, her face a neutral mask. The door clicked and opened.

"Richard?" she said.

"Hey, sweets," he said, dragging in a bag over his shoulder. He hugged her, took in Martin. "I didn't know you were coming. What are you guys doing up anyway?"

They stared at him.

Martin said, "Where'd you go?"

"Didn't you get the flowers?" Richard asked, touching Elizabeth on the wrist. "Bloody hell. I'm sure they charged me for them."

"What flow—"

He opened the door and looked out on the stoop, then slammed it shut. "Maybe . . . ," he said, and strode through the kitchen and out into the living room. They just stood there as the back door opened and they could hear him leave and he came back as quickly as he left and wagged a bulkily wrapped vase at them. "Here they are! They were left out back. Now, why the hell do you suppose they did that?"

She tore them open and read the card, passed it to Martin. *Had to get out for a few days, Sweets. Back by Sunday. Richard.*

"I was in Amsterdam," he said.

"She knew that." Martin smiled. But there was something a little off—no date on the card, just the ease of it all. It didn't smell right.

"I guessed it," Elizabeth managed. "But I thought—"

"I'd left?" He nuzzled her and grinned. "Not this boy." He rubbed the back of his neck. "I'm knackered, though. Should we get some sleep?"

"Let's," she said.

They started up the stairs.

"Oh, and Martin," he said back over his shoulder, "I brought back some really good stuff."

"That's great," Martin said. "I can't wait."

He sat in the living room with one lamp lit, trying to remember. Hadn't he been out back with trash or recyclables? Hadn't he seen that gate? It was hard for him to believe they'd stood there for three days, unnoticed. Had it rained? Had it been too cold? In the kitchen he peered at them. They looked pretty damn good for being out in the March weather. But he couldn't have picked them up this late. Unless he'd carried them back from Holland. That probably wasn't allowed, was it? It was hard to believe that she'd had no sense of this particular possibility, that he hadn't brought himself to at least call, that he could look so damn smug and prepared at four in the fucking morning, that he could so blithely sense their shock.

And why had he come back—why would anyone come back—to this? Was he just another guy who needed to get out and have a little fun before returning to the relentlessness? There was something else, something vague and yet certain. He'd come back as if he'd never really left; but he'd gone, all right. He'd always had a quality of separateness about him, and he'd separated himself. It was something beyond his Britishness, his yoga and course work. An innate and eerie distance. Had Martin ever seen him close? He doubted it.

On his way to his own room, he stood for an instant— an eye blink—at their door. They were talking in low, soothing voices to each other. What did he know anyway? He really didn't know what anything was like between them, how often—or if—they could have sex, what they talked about when no one else could hear, what—or if— they thought when they chanted, what they thought about all this. Everybody died. But what went on between now and then—all the entanglements and annoyances and deprivations and enjoyments and inspirations and despair and redemption—you could never really know unless it was you or the person came right out and told you, and even in the telling there'd have to be a shift between what it was and what language made it sound like it was. Could nothing be shared? He wished he were back in his own bed with his own screaming thoughts and fears and dreams. He wished he were younger, he wished he were older. He wished that his wife could tell him everything she ever thought, and he wished that he'd be interested by all of it. He wished he didn't ache for a hundred different women. He wished that his kids would stop growing up, and he wished that they were already grown up and done and safe and out of the house. He wished that his father were dead, and he wished that his father were once again young enough that he could actually talk with him. Had he ever really talked with his father? And what the hell did that mean—*really talk*? Did anyone really talk? Did anyone really listen?

As he lay in bed, he heard the click of doors and got up and peeked out into the hall. The bathroom light was on, the door cracked open. He stepped lightly along the carpet. She was standing at the mirror, her face so close it looked like she was trying to see inside herself. He noticed how narrow and delicate her shoulder blades were, how thin her waist was, how the hollows above her calf muscles at the backs of her knees seemed slightly more indented, slightly more defined. Her bare elbows reminded him of how they used to tear and gouge at each other when they were kids, banging into cabinets, slamming into the refrigerator and nearly toppling it. Once they had a race from the bottom of the driveway up to the garage and inside it to the glass storm door of the kitchen, and he'd been so desperate to win that he'd gone *through* the kitchen door, glass exploding around him. At first she'd cried and then, when she saw he was unmarked, she'd laughed until she couldn't breathe.

Now he waited for her to turn, but she was putting so much pressure on herself that she could sense nothing else. He felt it in his own chest, how hard she was trying, he felt it the way he felt all the weaknesses and traps of his own body whenever he thought of hers. Elizabeth, I'm here, he wanted to say. But he turned from the door.

In the morning or around noon or whenever it was when he woke, the house sounded empty. Vacated. Stilled.

"Hello," he called cautiously from his bed.

He couldn't hear anything. The room was terribly bright. He'd forgotten to close the window dressing. He'd forgotten to shut the door. He'd forgotten that when he woke he'd still be here. His chest wasn't as tight as the night before, but it was still pretty damn tight. He got out tentatively and rested his feet on the floor. Odd how one set of toenails was clear and crisp, and the other set looked like it had been dipped in yellow chalkdust. He'd been falling apart for years. He had to get home.

As far as he could tell, their convertible was missing from the street. Downstairs was only the blank kitchen—not even a note, not even a dirty glass or a piece of silverware in the sink. He dug out the phone book and called the airline. They kept him on hold for forty-five minutes. Forty-six. Forty-seven. Incredible. He'd already missed the day's flights. Finally they let him on the first one tomorrow.

He hunted for his copy of the house key. It wasn't where he swore he'd left it. Fucking Richard probably took it. Where the hell was that coming from? He was sorry he had to make the damn trip again. He felt like he was always the one being pulled by a string. He was sorry about that, too.

In the backyard he stared up at their patch of clouds and listened for noise from other backyards, but there was only the emptiness of everyone off at work or out to lunch. Beyond walls a cat growled, and soon he saw it stepping along the top of Richard's latticework. He stared at the cat and the cat stared at him.

What was he so unhappy about? He loved his wife, his kids; he was still alive; there was nothing he knew of that was wrong with him or them. He *hadn't* known Jane Wilson. He couldn't protect Elizabeth from whatever she was enduring. He could only be with her, and if she would rightly rather be with Richard, then wasn't he finally cut loose from all this? But he loved her.

In the study he started up the computer. He could occupy himself. Eventually she would call or come back. And tomorrow he would, for a moment, get to leave. He had more balance than he knew.

S h e c o o k e d Sarah breakfast while Max spent one of his TV tickets, then she made his breakfast while Sarah dressed, and she got Max dressed while Sarah whined about her hair, and by quarter to nine she had them both out the door, ferried the girl across the street to school, strapped Max in the car seat and hauled him to Stepping Stones. At nine o'clock she was in her office. So far so good. She had to teach Martin's three classes between ten and two-thirty, and then pick up Sarah by three-fifteen. She could do it. She was doing it.

The e-mails to Martin that he asked her to check were all cautionary, professional, and legalistic. He was not to speak about Jane Wilson, period. With the infanticide there had been phases of secrecy and interrogation, but even if Martin had sensed the student's depression, who was he anyway? He was just an anthropology professor. Some schools didn't even have anthropology.

She stiffened herself for the first class. He'd told her what the last one had been like. Yesterday she had been out raking the lawn, and their neighbor had stopped over, a college alum in his seventies who had returned, almost salmonlike, to this town to retire. Now he was bereft. "We didn't have this when we were their age," he said, his face mottled with sorrow. "This self-confidence problem or whatever you call it." Self-esteem, she suggested. "Yeah, well, whatever. We didn't kill ourselves back then." She had stepped back and looked at him calmly, the children out of earshot in a pile of leaves. "People have always been killing themselves," she said. "Well, don't you two people go getting depressed or anything," the neighbor said, his face rosaceous. "It's not worth it."

"Lauren?"

It was Ruben. "Hi," she said.

"Isn't Martin in today?"

She told him, as tersely as she could, Martin's situation while he lounged in the doorway and kept pulling out a cigarette from a nearly crumpled pack and shoving it back in again.

"Well, do you have a phone number for him? They're going to have to talk to him."

She gave it to him. "Anything else?"

"Nope," he said. He shut the door.

She was lifting the phone to call him when it rang in her hand. The vibration made her drop it. It rang again. All right.

"Hello," she said.

"Hey." It was him.

"Ruben's going to call you. They need to talk with you some more."

"Richard came back," he said.

"What?"

"Last night. Very late. Weird. And now the car is gone and neither of them are here."

"When you coming home?"

"Tomorrow."

She sighed happily. "Hey, that's great!"

He told her again which disks had the assignments. "So, how are you anyway?" he asked.

"How are you?"

"I can't wait to get home."

"Me, too."

He paused. "Their call waiting. I've got to take it."

"Call us."

"I will."

She set the phone on the hook. What a relief that Richard had returned. She hadn't thought he'd stay away for long, but it was impossible to know. She couldn't blame him. After all this she never wanted to blame anybody for anything, she wanted to move forward. She knew that was naive. She liked naiveté. It made her feel restful. Or rested.

She printed out the assignments and was about to make the necessary photocopies when the phone rang again.

"Yes?" she said.

"That wasn't Ruben, it was Elizabeth," Martin said, his voice tense. "They'll be home so late they don't know whether they'll see me, and I should just wake them in the morning to say good-bye."

"Maybe they just need the time alone," she said gently.

"Maybe I just get the fuck out of here today."

"You can't."

"I know. I know."

He was silent while she watched the minutes evaporate before his class.

"I've really got to do these copies," she said.

"All right. I'll call you."

Annka stood in the hall right outside Lauren's office door, as if she'd been lurking.

"Is everything all right?" she asked daintily. "Is Martin upset?"

Lauren stared at her. "Everything is fine."

At least she'd told him where the key was. He had it now as he walked up the street toward the tube stop. Almost half the day left. He tried to lift himself. London. He could do anything! He kicked at a chunk of broken beer bottle and gave a whistle. The air was cold, the sky was clearing. London!

The high street clattered and chinked with traffic and trash. He bought a day pass from one of the machines and headed into town. Hamley's was in the middle of another refurbishment, and he had a terrible time finding the right aisles and once in them finding anything suitable. It was always easier at the airport, when he had only a few minutes and the stores offered only a few choices.

He bought Sarah a set of special drawing pencils that she probably already had, and he found for Max what must have been his seventeenth or eighteenth tractor. Twenty pounds spent, just like that.

On the street again, he pulled up short. Maybe Richard was mad about him being there. Maybe he was tired of being constantly mistrusted and of having Martin drop in at any hint of crisis. Maybe that was it. Suddenly he felt a little better.

He found a set of coffee mugs that looked like they were made in Italy but were actually from China, painted with vines of purple grapes and bold blue and yellow and orange stripes, narrow at the base and wide at the rim. Lauren would like them, and they were only another twelve pounds.

He had no idea where to drink, and now everyone seemed to be heading out for one. In previous trips he and Richard had always been allowed out once or twice, and they always went to terrific pubs or free houses, where the beer was incredible and they'd have hopeful conversations about all the traveling they wanted to do and there were even girls to look at. He recalled one place that had picnic tables on the sidewalk that caught the last of the day's sun, and when they'd moved inside the lights were warm and they sat at huge butcher-block tables, and for some reason or another a few girls joined them and they talked and laughed until they announced they had to go back to their wives. Where the hell was that place?

He always felt that London was the kind of town

where you couldn't just walk and find something, you had to know where you were going. Like most parts of New York. He'd never lived in either city. He'd only visited. He was a hick from the hinterlands. God, he felt good. God, he felt happy.

He sat at the first bar drinking something dark. Elizabeth had sounded a little tense, a little distant, and now he knew why. He'd involved himself between them. What a jerk he was. He wished he'd thought of telling her that on the phone. But she'd been so . . . dismissive, almost. "Go out and have some fun," she'd said. He'd just gone along and allowed himself to be dismissed. Just another way in a series of ways that he'd been swallowing parts of himself ever since she'd told him she was ill. Not well. Whatever she called it.

On the wall the bar menu bragged the usual English crap. He ordered another of the same—stout or porter, he'd forgotten which—and tried to think of a good neighborhood between here and Dunkers Green. He liked Hampstead, but Hampstead was at least a couple of changes away on the tube. Findlay had that new mall, but there'd be nothing to look at while he drank. He didn't even know how to get to Chelsea, and there was no way that place was anywhere near the right direction. But it was his last night in London! He gulped the beer and sauntered from the pub.

The 7-Eleven had lots of recognizable cigarette brands, even his favorite. He felt like anything could happen now. He had a little money and an excellent credit card. Wasn't alcohol a depressant? Why did it always make him so goddamn happy?

At Hampstead—yes, Hampstead, to his wonder he'd made it, a gray-and-yellow blur of getting on and off trains and going up and down escalators trying not to read the ads posted alongside—there were almost too many good places to choose from and he felt a wonderful determination to try them all. He hadn't cut loose like this in a long time. And it was still daylight. London!

He nursed another dark one at a picnic table not far from the curb, and watched the people and the traffic pass, a lot of miniskirts on kind of a cold day. At other tables everyone seemed to be eating fries. He smoked two or three cigarettes, feeling healthier and more invincible with each one, and to his surprise ordered another beer. He'd been sure he'd be moving on by now. The beer was colder and thicker and just better than the last, but it was the same beer. Well, it was just better. This was his . . . fourth? Fifth? Fourth. He'd been at it for just over two and a half hours, including whatever it took to get here. He'd better pace himself, or he'd be home by nine with nothing better to do than watch the walls spin and channel surf with only four or five stations to look at. Four or five.

Bread. Something to soak it all up. He nodded his thanks inside to the bartender and walked soberly next door to a take-out pizza place and wolfed down a slice. Or was it a take-out pierogi place and was he quaffing a knish?

He sat on a bench attached to the entrance of the heath, although the actual heath was, he knew, incredibly far away and a little uphill and then downhill and then uphill from where he sat. Was it too late to slow down?

Was the night already over for him? It didn't seem fair. He'd drink water but it would only make him drunker. Somebody had taught him that. Lauren? Lauren.

He hiked down the long high street, trying to be pleasant, to get sober. Four pints. That translated into a six-pack. That was a night's work. He'd really love to try somewhere else, but he didn't want to sit there being all stupid and nauseous and drooling, trying to hide how much saliva he'd have to be spitting out every two or three minutes. Too bad he'd wasted the night. Too bad he didn't have more self-control. Too bad he had never grown up. What was he thinking sitting down in that basement getting stoned? What was he thinking drinking as much as he drank? How pathetic. How irresponsible. How narcissistic.

He walked until he was nearly okay and then went into a really cool place—high ceilings, regal moldings, tall brassy mirrors, low chairs, marble tables, mahogany bar. You wouldn't want to leave anything out when describing a place like this. Peanut shells on the floor. Life-size papier-mâché creatures posted in elevated nooks and crannies. Cute waitresses. Lots of girls at the tables and one or two at the bar. A place where he was in danger of being the oldest person. But there was an old bald guy sitting alone in a corner, smoking a goddamn pipe. God, he was bald himself. Sometimes he forgot. He wondered why. Maybe he had too much self-esteem. Maybe he just never saw himself as bald, even when he looked in the mirror. Every now and then he'd see a picture of himself from the worst angle and be shocked. Just shocked.

Straight on, face-to-face with a looking glass, it was hard to see himself that way. But from slightly above, like from where one of those papier-mâché guys sat eyeing him, it was impossible to conclude otherwise. He was really bald, like someone had just sawed off the entire top of his head.

"Sir?"

God, he had a flight tomorrow—god, he had to be at the airport by nine fucking o'clock, and he hadn't even ordered a car yet. Elizabeth said the card for the service was on the—-

"Beer," he heard himself say.

"Beer?" Was she smirking at him? Why did women bartenders have to wear such tight T-shirts? "What kind of beer?"

"Something dark," he said. "I've been drinking dark other places, and I shouldn't switch. Actually I probably shouldn't even switch between darks, but it's too late for that." He felt a need to spit and choked it back.

"Something dark," she laughed at him. She was laughing at a bald man. How incredibly rude.

"You know. Not light. Not yellow. Not orange or amber or tin—" Tin? "Brown," he said. "But not choco-late, not maple. I can't stand sweet beer." He pulled out his pack of cigarettes and pulled out a cigarette and dropped it on the floor and had to descend like some kind of mountain climber from his bar stool and bend forward farther than he'd ever bent before to pick it up, all the while shining everyone his precious glaring meek bald head, and then reascend to find her looking at him, mirthful or snide he couldn't tell.

"You're not driving?" she said.

"Tubing," he said.

That seemed to settle it and she brought him a really dark beer. It tasted like anchovies. No, that wasn't right. It tasted like Guinness. Sadly, he shook his head at himself.

"Is it not all right?"

God, she had a cute accent. Then again, he was in fucking England. "It's terrific," he said with too much enthusiasm.

She smiled. "Works on you guys every time."

"I know." He was sad again.

"First time in London?"

"Nope." He looked from side to side. For some reason he was the only guy sitting at the bar, where two pairs of girls were sitting elbow to elbow, smoking furiously. He managed to light his cigarette.

"Just seems it, then," the bartender said. She seemed to like smiling at him. Maybe people liked smiling at bald men.

"I've had too much to drink," he said.

She lightly touched her hand to her cheek. "I had no idea." She mopped the counter in front of him with an almost-white rag. He swallowed more spit.

"I'm not a tourist," he said, puffing his cigarette, then taking a shallow sip of his beer. "I'm visiting family." He put down his cigarette. " 'Scuse me," he said, feeling green. "Where is—"

"Round back," she said, excusing him. "You'd better hurry."

As he splashed water on his face, he tried to count back to the last time he'd done this to himself. He didn't think he'd been this stupid since before Max was born, so that was at least three years back—the little guy was almost three. Was it when he'd gone to give that paper in San Francisco and Lauren had stayed behind with Sarah, and he'd met all his graduate school buddies for scotch and beers and martinis and shots of tequila? Was it that time in Atlanta that Lauren had taken Sarah to visit her mother and he'd gone out with some fathers of Sarah's preschool friends and they'd hit a dozen different bars downtown, and he'd had rum drinks and vodka drinks and rum drinks again and then capped it with some amber beer and Percodan? The rumor was Jane Wilson never drank or smoked or took anything stronger than iced tea. The rumor was that she'd gone from shop to shop and found the rope at a paint store, that the chair pocked the wall in her dorm room when she kicked it back. That—conversely—she'd been murdered instead of having taken her life.

When he came out with his face scrubbed by a dozen wet paper towels and sweat in pronounced lines at the backs of his knees and down each underarm, he saw his place at the bar had been emptied and neatened.

"Back from the dead already?" the bartender said.

He nodded tentatively. "I'd like to pay."

"It's not necessary." She reached over and patted him maternally on the shoulder. "Just take better care of yourself. Right?"

"Yes," he said, already turning for the door. "Thank you. Yes."

How he made it home he hoped he would never recall. The thing was that long after he'd expected it, he was finally climbing up the stairs at Dunkers Green and gaining the sidewalk not three blocks from their rowhouse, and it wasn't even ten o'clock and the streets were still gritty with the day's crap. He stepped through it and down the long, long residential block and made the right turn, something inside his head just hammering away at his temple—hammer, hammer, hammer—and there at last was their place, and he had the key in the door and opened it and shut it quickly after him and pounded up the stairs to his beloved ibuprofen and took three with an enormous glass of water and threw himself on the bed and hoped for sleep.

"We're home," she called to the backseat triumphantly as she wheeled the car into the driveway. Sarah said something disdainful, and Max merely grinned and nodded his head. "What a day, huh?"

She pressed the garage-door opener and watched the wide, heavy door begin its slow rise up into the ceiling. A foot off the ground it stopped. It was temperamental like that. She pressed the clicker again, and the door sunk back to the concrete drive. Max whined.

"One minute," she said. "Sometimes you have to hit it twice."

She hit it again, and again the door rose grudgingly from the cement, and three feet off the driveway again it stopped, only this time it was crooked, as if the whole house were listing into the ground.

"Uh-oh," she said.

"Uh-oh?" Max said. "What's uh-oh?"

"The garage door," Sarah said.

"Not working?" Max said.

"Exactly."

"Wait here." Lauren got out from the car and walked slowly to the door. She didn't want that thing coming down on her. It hung at a twenty-degree angle about waist-high off the ground. She wouldn't touch it. It looked like a kind of guillotine.

"At least the car's out and safe," she told the children back in the car. She hit the clicker again. The door didn't budge. Now the damn thing wouldn't even go down. Shoot. "All right," she said. "Let's go in."

She went around and got Max and his schoolbag out of the car and made sure Sarah got herself out without any incident and they trooped up the breezeway stairs, she unlocked the door, and now they were inside.

"TV?" Max said.

"Okay," she said. "Okay." She turned to Sarah. "Can you guys get settled in front of the TV while I see about the door?"

"Will you stay inside?" Sarah pouted.

"Yes, I'll be inside. Now go on."

She waited until she could hear the TV and then she pulled out the phone book and looked under Garage and then Garage Builders and then Doors and Gate Operating Devices and actually found something called Potterstown Overhead Door and called and arranged a service visit. Quietly she ducked into the breezeway and eyed the car. Windows up. Doors locked.

It was a little late to call Martin but it wasn't too late and besides he'd said that Elizabeth and Richard would be out all evening. She let it ring and ring. When the answering machine picked up on the seventh or eighth time, she was relieved. He'd be furious about the door. She dug out the homeowner's policy and checked to see if the item was covered. In boldface they made sure she knew it wasn't.

While the noodles and broccoli cooked, she emptied the dishwasher and put everything away and checked Sarah's schoolbag for various notes and announcements and the homework assignment and bagged the trash and put it on the breezeway and set the table. She drained the noodles and made one bowl with olive oil and parmesan and another bowl with pesto and arranged the broccoli on an oval plate that the kids liked and put a cup of ice water at each of the three places.

"Dinner," she called.

Sarah came and sat at her place, and Lauren helped her to the pesto pasta and the broccoli and then served herself and sat watching happily as Sarah began to eat. It was always wonderful to watch either of them eat, as if some miracle was happening. When they were babies neither took a bottle and it was always just her and her breasts, and even when they moved on to rice cereal and all the little jars they still favored breast milk. She'd breast-fed them each for eighteen months, and Martin argued that if it hadn't been so long the transition might have been easier, but he just felt left out. Martin. He was probably on the town—a quaint phrase—knowing him, alone with nothing to do. She hoped he didn't end up regretting it too much.

"Max!" she said loudly.

No answer. She looked at Sarah and Sarah shrugged.

"Max, it's dinner!" Lauren shouted.

"Not yet," Max said.

"Oh brother," Sarah said.

"Don't," Lauren said. She sighed and got up from her chair and walked into the living room. The cartoon crime-fighters show was almost over. She waited. When the credit roll started, she picked up the remote and turned off the TV.

"Hey!" Max said. "I want to see the credit roll."

She was amazed he even knew the term. "It's dinner-time," she said.

"I WANT TO!"

"All right, all right. But just the credit roll." She switched it back on, and he wagged his shoulders and squirmed his butt to the music. At last it was over. She switched off the TV again. "Now dinner," she said.

"Okay. Okay." He trooped into the kitchen as if on a forced march and climbed up on his chair and looked at his plate, while she delicately arranged a bit of the parmesan noodles and some broccoli. "Yuck," he said.

"Honey, it's one of your favorites."

"Don't want it."

Sometimes she would let herself be pushed into get-ting up and making something else. "This is what we have," she said firmly.

"Yuck," he said again.

Sarah laughed with her mouth full and shards of pasta sprayed on her plate. Max giggled.

"Dessert?" he asked.

"When you eat your dinner."

"Yuck," he said. He picked a noodle from the pile, inspected it suspiciously, and ate it. Sarah drank water and began on her food again. In the silence Lauren lifted her fork. That hadn't been so difficult, and now she had a nice view of her two children eating and the new bookcases gleaming at her from the living room.

Then the house shuddered as if it had been slammed against a wall. Her fork dropped on the table. They were all out of their chairs, staring at one another, moving at once to the breezeway, squeezing through the door, her head ringing, a new migraine just beginning to express itself behind her left eye.

"Don't go in," she hissed, holding them back from the garage.

They went out the breezeway door into the driveway. In the distance a fire alarm sounded, as if someone had already called for their rescue. The garage door sagged and buckled into the pavement, as if it had been brought to its knees. Cracks spread in glaring webs up its spine and along its edges; flakes of paint were littered on the driveway.

"Wow," she said, holding the children away from it.

"What happened?" Max said.

"It fell and broke itself," Sarah said. "Or first it broke, and then it fell and broke some more. Right, Mommy?"

"Right," Lauren said. The siren seemed to be in her head, but she knew it was nowhere near.

"Why?" Max asked.

"Because," Lauren said, "sometimes things just fall apart."

"And break?" Max said.

"And break," she said.

The beeping was stunning him, just stunning him as it pelted him with the gleeful fact that he'd even managed to set the alarm. He was getting up, moving expertly to turn off the noise, no hangover in sight. What luck! He didn't deserve such luck. But there was something. Shit. Now he was wide-awake, out of bed, in his underwear, moving to the door. He'd forgotten to order a car.

Downstairs in the cold morning light he paged through the business cards and found the one, hustled to the phone in the kitchen, dialed.

"Morning," a voice said.

"Is it possible," he started, his voice cracking into dry little pieces of hungover hoarseness, even though he still had no headache. "Is it possible to still order a car for Heathrow?"

"Yes," the voice said languidly, "I suppose it's possible."

"In forty minutes?"

"I don't see why not."

"In Dunkers Green?"

"Certainly."

"Wonderful," he said, his voice now rising, then shutting itself down as he remembered the sleeping people upstairs. Quietly he gave the address.

Now he even, unbelievably, had time for a shower. He

hurried up to his room, found a clean set of clothes, and poured himself into the bathroom. He let the shower beat him for a while with its thudding heat. They had much better pressure here. Then he got dressed and brushed his teeth, tried not to whistle as he packed his bag, took it downstairs and set it by the door. He checked outside. The car was already waiting. He still had five minutes. He took the stairs two at a time and tapped lightly on their door.

No answer.

He tapped again and opened it soundlessly. The bed was empty. Still made. He looked around quickly. They hadn't ever come home. Shit. He remembered hearing ringing last night. He raced downstairs. No message on the machine.

Outside, the car still waited.

He scrawled *I'll call from the airport. What happened?* At the front door he tried to remember how to set the alarm, punched in numbers, heard the damn thing beep earnestly, shut it down, and shut himself from the house, the key inside. He felt a pang at that. In a minute he was opening the back door of the little compact and squeezing in.

"Sorry," he muttered.

"What?" the driver said, turning to look at him, an older guy with an indifferent face.

"Never mind," he said.

"Is it Heathrow, then?"

He settled back in the seat, the hangover flooding him with nausea, regret, and ache. "Yes," he said.

They chugged down the lane. These services always took the most roundabout and clogged route. He shut his eyes and willed himself to sleep. Where the hell were they? Maybe having a special night at a hotel? Richard was too cheap for that. Not even a message. Maybe they just got stuck somewhere. They would have taken a taxi home. That had to be cheaper than a hotel. He rattled the pence in his pocket, making sure he had change for the call. At least he had gifts for everyone. Pockets of air flung themselves around inside his empty stomach. The restaurant at the airport was so crappy. Where the hell were those guys?

The car seemed to be strolling through the bleakest neighborhoods, two-story houses jammed up against one another along barren streets clotted with parked cars, the occasional convenience store just opening its shutters to show off its stacks of tins and boxes. Standstill places. It would be so nice to get home, where there were grass and trees and a fireplace, the kids would nuzzle him and he'd even pet the cats. Do you even know where you are? someone said.

"What?" he said.

"What?" the driver said, without turning back.

"Nothing," he said.

Finally they were on the only bit of highway that the damn service was willing to take. Could he sleep? Forget it.

At Heathrow he overtipped, pushing for some karma. He found a pay phone and called. The answering machine. What to do, what to do. He just had a bad feeling.

It was only four in the morning back home. If he

called Lauren now, she'd probably reach across the ocean and throttle him.

He had an hour before he absolutely had to check in. He called them every ten minutes, watching his pence run out. He was probably just being paranoid, or suffocating. Or hangover stupid. Lauren would know. He gave up and dialed.

It rang all four times and the machine picked up, and then he heard her voice through his own taped voice *You've reached the home of Martin, Lauren, . . .* "Hello? Hello?" she was saying. "What is it? What is it?" as if she had to say everything twice to hear that it was herself who was actually talking.

"It's me," he said. "From Heathrow."

"What?"

"You told me to call. Remember?"

"I didn't mean it," she said.

"What?"

"You know, not this early. You never call this early. You call around seven. Before takeoff. Around then. Don't you?"

"They never came back."

"Who?"

"Elizabeth and Richard."

"Oh." She swallowed loudly and took a breath into the phone. For some reason he imagined her breath smelled quite bad, and he winced. "So?" she said.

"Don't you think it's weird?"

"They probably just wanted to have some privacy," she said.

"She didn't even call," he said.

"Yes she did. You told me she did."

"She didn't call *again,*" he said.

"She has to call more than once?" She yawned even more loudly than she swallowed.

"Christ," he said.

"So." She was trying to wake up. "Is your flight on time?"

"Yes, I have to check in."

"Well, then go check in."

"You're not getting this at all." He heard the anger in his voice and stopped himself.

"Getting what? Maybe you're not explaining it at all. Maybe you're just making something out of nothing. Maybe you had too much to drink last night, and you have no idea what's going on."

"Shut up!" he roared.

"I'm hanging up," she said.

"Lauren," he said. "Lauren, please. I need your help here."

"Well, then don't tell me to shut up. You hate being told to shut up. People tell you to shut up and you just freak out."

"I'm glad you're awake," he said.

"Listen," she said. "They're two adults. They can do whatever they want to do."

"I know," he said. "I know. It's just . . ."

"What? Come on, honey. I want to try to get back to sleep. I have to *teach,* you know."

"The way he came back from out of nowhere. And

now they're both gone. I don't think I should leave until I at least talk to her again."

"That is so illogical," she said. "They could have decided to go on one of those retreats. Or to get away somewhere. She'll call when she wants to call."

"It doesn't feel right."

"*You* don't feel right. *Its* can't feel."

"HONEY!"

"Okay—oh shit. I think I hear Max."

Oh Christ, he'd somehow gone and woken Max. "I'm sorry. So look, can I stay?"

"*Can* you stay? You can do whatever you want. That's what this whole thing has been about, trying to figure out just what it is you *want* to do about . . . about all this." She stopped, and he could hear Max saying something in the background. "You want to say hi to Daddy?"

"Look—"

"He doesn't want to say hi. But he said you are a beautiful skier. What do you suppose that means?"

"So I'm gonna wait and see," he said.

"Honey, please. Haven't you been saying how sick you are of giving yourself up over this? I mean, you want to do the right thing, but you don't know what the right thing is. Nobody does. Nobody ever does. Just get on the plane. That's the right thing for now. And later there will be another right thing."

"I'm going to wait," he said resolutely.

"Martin. Oh, he's gotta go pee. Yes, honey, here we go. Martin, just call me, all right? I'm not the one right now you need to talk to. Okay?"

"Okay," he said.

"But of course you can stay. Do whatever you want about this. I just think you're being . . . like your mother," she said. And hung up.

Oh, that was cruel. But her tone had no edge to it.

He found a rest room and urinated and stood at the sink. He took off his glasses and splashed water on his face. Now he felt kind of alert.

At the counter he gave up his ticket and passport.

Has anyone you know . . . ?

To your knowledge . . .

He got his aisle seat, but in the last row. He'd be sniffing the lavatory fumes the whole damn flight. Through customs he felt the nausea again welling in his throat. He wandered over to the specialty scotch shop. They were pouring free shots of something that should have looked tasty, but his stomach recoiled. Free shots of a single malt, and he couldn't even do it. Every time he left Heathrow he felt ill, empty, just sick and unstable. As if he were doing someone harm and he didn't quite know who it was. Elizabeth? Himself? He always wanted to take himself out of any equation that involved her. Leaving was selfish. He got to leave. She couldn't. Not even Richard really could. Or maybe he could.

He tried the phone again, heard the machine, hung up, went and sat in one of those racks of chairs stuck in the middle of the floor.

His plane was called. He still had thirty actual minutes. It wasn't right. It wasn't right to go like this. It wasn't right that anybody had to be the sick one. It wasn't right that Lauren would be stuck on the other side with the kids and all the teaching. It wasn't right that he felt like the damn pivot, that he had any feelings at all.

In his plastic seat in the long yellow tube he tried to imagine what they were like now, where they were, but he couldn't see them. There wasn't some mental trick to it, he couldn't project it, it wasn't there. The only thing there was the rattle of the tracks, the glum, everyday, indifferent faces of people who made this haul six or seven days a week, in from Heathrow, out to Heathrow, chugging here and there. Mind the gap. He couldn't get into the gap.

He reached Dunkers Green by two. Past lunchtime. He'd forgotten to eat anything yet. Was there stuff in the fridge? At their house he rang the bell, knowing it would do no good. Then he went around to the alley with the seven-foot-tall wooden gate and climbed over it and then tested the side door into the laundry room—locked—and then went into the backyard, roughly the size of the living room and kitchen, and examined the French double doors and tried to remember how they might be locked. It was a complicated system of dead bolts into the floor and frame, but the floor dead bolt was worn away and often when he had tried to lock it it didn't hold. The top bolt was more difficult. He didn't want to break the entire door.

Then it began to rain.

Why hadn't he kept the key? After all, he'd had an intuition, an inkling, a kind of frisson. He *knew*. As the rain filled the natural hush of the space where the block's backyards met, he dug around in the stony fringe of the patio, found the meatiest rock, pulled down his jacket sleeve around his hand, held the rock through it, and, as he crushed it into the pane beside the door handle, he still heard himself thinking, Do I really have to do this? Do I?

The glass was far thicker than he'd thought—after all, it was the only glass separating inside from outside—and the pane gave with all the brittleness of a brick wall. He'd made only an uncomplicated map of cracks. His hand hurt, but didn't seem to be bleeding. He felt dizzy. Beside him his briefcase was beginning to shine and wither with rain. He reached back again with the rock, and with all his force drove his hand toward the cracked glass. It shattered into different shards—some, he could feel, embedding themselves through his coat sleeve into his knuckles—and gave way to an eight-inch square opening into the kitchen.

Through the rush of water and pain he thought he heard someone calling to him.

"Yes, you, you bloody fucking idiot!" a man shouted from an upstairs window in the next house. "What the hell do you think you're doing!"

"She's my sister," he screamed back through the rain.

"Bloody hell! Stay where you are!" His head left the window, and Martin stayed in the rain, afraid to look at how quickly his blood was soaking through his jacket, impaling himself on a mixture of disbelief and pain. He *was* a bloody fucking idiot. An impulse to run shivered through him. But where? Why? He kicked his sopping briefcase tight against the wall and kept it there with his nylon travel bag. Everything was soaked. Still, he wouldn't look at his hand. He glanced out past the end of the backyard, the rain a curtain between him and the rest of Dunkers Green.

"Their brother?" A large, oafish man stood in the door of the kitchen, staring him down. "Is that what you said you were?"

"Yes," he said.

"You have any identification?" He blocked the doorway and laughed. "Only kidding. Of course I've seen you around. You might as well come in. That's what you're after, isn't it?"

"Yes." Martin threw his bags in heavily and ducked in, and the lout shut the doors.

"I had a key." He held it out to show Martin.

"Of course," Martin said.

"Don't they do this sort of thing in America?"

"They do. They do." He felt something dripping and looked down at the floor. Drops of blood mingled in with slivers of glass.

"You must feel pretty stupid." He started toward the front of the house. "You coming?"

Martin staggered, a bit light-headed, after him. "Where to?" he mumbled.

"The hospital," he said, opening the front door for him. "After you."

He'd never been that good about blood or pain, and in the car he alternated between a swoon and a desire to puke. He felt his face going whiter and whiter. They were in one of those cars that looked like half a car, their knees practically jammed up into their chins, rain seeping through the supposedly shut tops of the windows.

"Is she at the hospital?" he said.

"Who?"

"My sister."

"Not to my knowledge. Is she sick, is she? I thought she was looking a little sick."

"Yes, she's sick."

"Not every day, of course. Just some days. Most days. What's she got?"

"Cancer."

"Oh."

They drove for a while in silence, Martin's mind seeming to fog and clear at once.

"I guess I actually thought it might be that. My mother had it. It's awful stuff." Martin felt him turn and look at him. He couldn't look back. "I suppose we all have it. That's what they say anyway. At the end of the day, we all have it."

Martin nodded.

"You over visiting? That's nice."

"Uh-huh."

"So where are they, then?"

"I have no idea," Martin said with finality, hoping that would shut him up.

"Think they needed a break?" He smacked Martin on

the knee. "Cancer is hell, you know. The tests, the treatments, the smells, the needles, the scans. Of course it's all a terrible cliché, except when it happens to you."

"I think I'm going to be sick."

"Oh?" He paused as if thinking that Martin might contract some cancer right there in the car. "Right!" He pulled over instantly, and Martin pushed and pulled at the door and stuck himself out in the rain and staggered to the sidewalk and frantically looked for something, anything, and there—right there—was an open bin, and into it he poured out what felt like his heart and brains.

A hand tenderly touched the back of his wet neck.

"There, there," the man said. "There, there."

It was hard for him to believe how long his life seemed to be going on.

Then he was back in the tight car, head thrown back as far as it could, holding his hand up as much as he could, the guy quietly urging him, "That's it, elevate. That's it, elevate," and the cars and the patterns he could see seemed to be crisscrossing through his head as if they were building him a whole new set of responses.

"Almost there," the guy said. "Do you think anything is broken?"

"I don't know," he said.

At the hospital they sat him in a padded chair and set his arm on some kind of arm desk or platform and snipped away the sleeve around the hand and soaked the wound and gently tweezered out the glass and soaked the wound some more. Or maybe it was more than one wound. He wouldn't look. At one point they gave him a shot of something, and at another point they stitched and sewed here and there, bits and bits of cuts, and the back of his hand when they were finally done looked like he'd spilled jam all over it and had mopped up only half. They wrapped it after telling him not to get it wet for a few days. The stitching would dissolve of its own accord. He could go home.

He paid with a credit card while the guy whom he absolutely did recall as the man who had rescued him from the rain stood alongside and double-checked the bill, whistling admiringly at the end, which was still not too bad and something Martin hoped his insurance back home would cover. Or maybe even the credit card company would cover it. He had no idea and he was too tired to think about the money, and besides, he really didn't want to.

The fat guy—he was fat—let him sit all stony eyed on the long ride back to the house. He let him in with a butlerian flourish and pushed him gently toward the stairs.

"Now, you get some rest," he said.

Martin nodded on his way up the steps. He still didn't know the guy's name, and he didn't want to. He laid himself on the bed. It was evening, sometime between six and midnight. He still hadn't eaten.

Within the darkness, he landed on a moment not long ago, when he was visiting, and Richard had made plans for them to go out to a long, elaborate dinner with a few Epiphany friends. But Martin could see Elizabeth wasn't up to it, and he told her they didn't have to do this and he would stay with her. And she shook her head, and her

yellowed face showed an appallingly unbearable determination as she said, "Oh, I'm going to go because I want
to be with him and he's going, and I hope it won't be too
long."

And months later, when she could not possibly endure
such an outing, how Richard would ask her to dress as if
she were going, just so he could see her that way.

Now it was dark and wet outside. Martin could envi-
sion them wandering through the night, but he couldn't
tell whether they were flinching and hunched or relaxed
and untouched or brazen and reckless. He couldn't tell
whether they were holding hands. They were so close
together, they seemed to disappear into one another at
the elbow. They were alone together in the wet dark.

" S o   y o u ' r e saying you really don't know when he'll be
back."

Lauren nodded her head and winced. "It's a weird situation. He needs to be over there."

"I can see that," Ruben said, clutching his beard. "I
can certainly see that. It's not like I don't understand.
But there's a lot of shit going on right now, and this is just
one more—"

"I think he'll be back soon," Lauren said.

"That's not the impression you just gave me. I mean,
what's *soon*, Lauren? Is soon next week? Is soon next
semester?"

"I think soon," she repeated.

"You know, I've got a lot of shit going on in my life,
too. I'm sure if we turned all our rocks over at the same

time, there'd be more worm-filled crap than we'd know what to do with. What's the difference between him sitting over there waiting for her and him sitting over here? That's what I don't get. I want to be reasonable. I'm glad you're meeting his classes. But for everyone's sake he should come home."

"Right," Lauren said.

"Did you know that Julia is in rehab again? Did you know that I had to take every fucking pill bottle and hide it? Did you know I can't even have aspirin in my own home? Did you know that we're in our forty-first year of marriage, and if rehab doesn't take this time it's going to be all over for us? And that fucking jerk David Lazlo is just abandoning his wife for a twenty-eight-year-old with two kids? I mean there's a lot of fucking shit going on, Lauren."

"I hear you," she said evenly.

"Maybe I'm just jealous because David and your husband are out there at least getting to deal with their shit full-time!"

"Martin isn't." Lauren felt herself blushing. "We're still here. We're part of it."

"Oh, yeah. Right. Sorry."

"Anyway, I've got to prep."

"Well." He turned in the doorway. "Good to talk to you. Keep me posted."

"I will. I will."

She watched the door slowly shut. The last few e-mails from Lazlo—from Kansas or wherever he was supposedly doing research, she could never tell which—always began with *My enemies are against me.* Of course, she kept replying, that's why they're called enemies. *I worry that Cindy is turning all my friends against me, too.* That she never bothered to respond to. The poor woman was in the midst of deciding on a hip replacement, and he was doing a twenty-eight-year-old? The whole department was now calling anything like it *Going to Kansas.* I heard David Lazlo went to Kansas. You think Ruben might go to Kansas? A few years back Chuck from Computer Science went to Kansas.

She wondered if Martin had ever considered going to Kansas.

Martin's family thought Richard had gone to Kansas.

Fifty percent of all marriages ended up in Kansas. Or had that dropped to forty? Or was that actually only divorce, and not definitely Kansas?

Her father said her mother had gone to Kansas. Her mother wouldn't talk about it. That was twenty-five years ago. It was hard to believe they still stirred it, poked at it, prodded it to keep it burning. They'd been perfect for each other, really. Same materialistic instincts, same compelling surfaces, same personality flaws. David Lazlo was smooth, but Cindy made him smoother. How could he have failed to see that?

Midlife crisis, they muttered around the department. Poor guy has a full weight room in his basement, drives that stupid Miata—you could see it coming from half a lifetime away. She knew people wrote him scolding e-mails, but at least all his lowly behavior was one form of being in charge of his own destiny. David Lazlo might be a jerk, but he was also a creature of desperation. That didn't make him evil. It just made him irresponsible, slightly unpredictable, and yet ultimately so transparent he seemed even more pathetic than usual. He had a half dozen of his own books on the shelf and a daughter who ran a New York ad agency and a red sports car and sabbatical every six years and one of the longest tenures at the college, and still he was pathetic. She knew he wanted to be noble. He was farther from it now than he had ever been. He must know that.

"Did you see it?"

It was Jane Doyle, their reclamation project, standing wryly in the door. Wryness was as close as she ever got to enthusiasm.

"What?"

"CNN. They're on the steps of White Hall. Doing something on 'The State of the American College.' The dead baby. Now the suicide. We're anthropological!"

Lauren rose, in either curiosity or dread, she couldn't tell which, and ventured to the window. Just one camera, just one reporter. Would they find out how weak everyone was? Wasn't everyone weak everywhere?

"Well," she said, turning to Jane and meeting her irony, "I guess that's something."

"Martin would love this," Jane said.

Now what? Martin was thinking. Now what. It was the next day, and he was still in bed trying not to hear the hammering and sawing that evidently was going on down in the kitchen.

He tried to move. It was amazing how one screaming hand could make everything else seem so impossible.

Imagine when his time came. He wouldn't be able to go anywhere. He'd be just pinned to the bed, waiting for whatever it was to finish him.

In the kitchen was the neighbor.

"You see?" he said, pointing with his saw as he knelt on the floor. "It's custom glass. The whole bloody door is custom-made. All I'm about doing is making up the missing panel with wood."

"Thank you," Martin said.

"You feeling all right? You look a little under it."

"Just fine," Martin said.

"There's the lad."

There were planks of wood on the kitchen floor with nails sticking up from them, as if the neighbor had been practicing. On the counter were plastic packets of bacon and ham, a tin of mackerel, a dozen eggs, and a liter of the kind of milk that didn't need to be refrigerated.

"Help yourself," the neighbor said. "I'll only be a minute here."

"Thank you," Martin said again.

The guy seemed to be sawing away at Martin's own stomach. At last he stopped and held up a perfect square and whistled. "That's the stuff," he said.

"Cheers," Martin said.

"Now the installation," the neighbor said, rising to eye the empty panel. "That's going to be tender business."

"Maybe we should—"

"Almost done," the neighbor said. He grabbed up some sandpaper from the counter and started in on the perfect square of wood. On the kitchen table were drills and bevels and a two-foot-long tool case so deeply gashed it looked like it had been through some kind of exploratory surgery. "It's not a big job," he said. "I just want to make sure, is all."

"Right," Martin agreed. He picked up a loaf of white bread, set it on a cutting board, and began to slice it with his left hand.

"Now, now." The neighbor dropped the sandpaper and wood and rushed over, took up the knife and loaf in his two meaty, sawdusty hands, and began to cut perfect one-inch slices. "This is the least I can do."

And then, in what seemed like a floury haze, he finished with the door, packed up his tools, and organized his lumber.

"You found a key, right?" he said.

"Yes." Martin blushed.

"Well, let me know if there's anything else you need help with."

"I will," Martin lied. "I will."

"I'm sure they'll turn up soon," the neighbor said.

When he'd gone, Martin sat at the empty kitchen table, letting the gratitude erode into general annoyance and then a soothing clarity. He was alone. He could think.

Maybe they would turn up soon. Maybe he was just being a fool.

Later, while it was still too early to really do anything, he found himself staring at the wall that separated him from the neighbor. There he lived and Martin had never seen him before, and it was easy to imagine he might not see him again. How many hundreds of times had Martin walked the street and never even known. The man's dignity. His courtesy. His humor. And he was gone to him again. There was comfort in that. And also something that made him feel dazed and uneasy, something mysterious, something mortal. Another guy with his own sufferings, his own life, his own nothingness.

Why the hell had he stayed? There was absolutely nothing he could do.

He couldn't bear to leave. It would be over if he left. He was just another guy sticking around at a crash site. They weren't ever coming back. His own sister. He just knew it. On top of everything else that he knew or could imagine, she was one of those stop-the-world-I-want-to-get-off types of people. Years ago he used to tease her that she wanted her life to be like a beer commercial. That got under her skin. When they were kids hoping for snow on New Year's Eve, she'd point out the window at the big flakes and say, Soon we'll be out there sledding with champagne. He'd never in his whole life sledded with champagne. When he was nineteen she took him tubing once on the Delaware. We'll rig up the beer in its own inner tube, she'd promised, and we'll just be drifting down the Delaware having our party. But the tubing service prohibited alcohol. For their honeymoon she and Richard had climbed glaciers in New Zealand, helicoptered, parasailed. She wasn't going to put up with this. She wasn't going to accept this. Who the hell should?

OUT OF
CONTROL

There were bills for the computer desk and the repainting of the study in "golden laughter," bills for ball therapy and cases of dozens of different vitamins, bills for wheatgrass deliveries and monthly colonics. Taped to the gold walls were index cards transcribed with what he took to be a guru's advice. *Straighten out your inner state. Clean the mirror of your heart. Focus on the purpose of your life. Believe in love.* On the shelves were books about how to get pregnant, how to get well, how to achieve balance, how to think. E-mails clinked in at a slow clip—they hadn't bothered to wall it off with a password—from strangers who didn't seem to suspect absence and from names dimly recognizable to him: Elizabeth's old high school friend whom he once had a crush on, a guy they had been in a car accident with twenty-five years ago on their way to Baskin-Robbin's in a rainstorm, a distant cousin who happened to be a nurse. Whenever the phone rang it was about a missed booking at this or that therapist, or a request that Richard or Elizabeth come pick up dry cleaning or a new wall hanging. Not an inkling from anyone that they might be gone. He sat on the swivel chair at the custom-built, three-thousand-dollar desk and swiveled as if one turn could take him around for a peek in India, Holland, upstate New York, California, and the time-share on Ibiza that they'd mentioned frequently. There were people whom he should call—Richard's parents and straitlaced sister, Richard's office. Instead, on the phone he spent time filling in holes for other people—her doctor, their mother, his wife—even though it was all one big hole to him. He'd been here now three or four days past the disappearance, and he had nothing new to report. The mail came. The gas-meter reader came.

It was too obvious, as Martin's mother conjectured, to think they were booked in with something as communal as the ashram or Epiphany. And maybe it was too naive, as he himself thought, to imagine that they would never come back. Oh, they'll come back, Martha and Lauren said. You should let them be.

He felt no instinct or pull that she needed to be rescued, that she wanted to be rescued, that rescue was possible. He felt only trapped by a void. Inside it he knew was just emptiness. But if he left, it would only grow larger and larger until he wouldn't even be able to define it again.

"It's pretty simple what you do," his mother said, once she had attained a reasonable calm. "You wait a month, and then you see what's on their credit card bills. Once they start having to charge stuff, we'll be able to find things out."

"They might have a lot of cash," Martin said.

"We could hire a detective."

"Don't you see my point?" he said.

"I am *not* losing my mind over this," his mother said.

"How's Dad?" he reminded himself to ask.

"He's good, he's good. He's doing great with the rehab. But it's hard getting used to—"

"The cancer?"

"No. The age," she said sadly, "just the age. The fact that he's seventy-three."

When he hung up, the phone rang again.

"Hey, kiddo."

It was Martha, her voice pitched to sympathy.

"Hey," he said.

"Don't you think you should just come home?"

"Not yet," he said.

"What exactly are you doing there anyway? I mean, are you calling around after them? What?"

"It's a little more complicated than that."

"You know, Martin, all of us are dealing with something. It's not just Elizabeth."

To that he had nothing to say.

"Your *wife* thinks you should come home."

"She's okay with it."

"Not really." She paused. "Think of your job. Think of your family."

He was going to try some calls to various authorities, he was going to visit Richard's office, he was going to call Richard's sister, he was going to get aggressive. Sometimes it hit him that if they wanted to be found they wouldn't be lost, and he felt the mire of inertia and doubt. He ought to go home. He ought to just get the fuck out of here. He ought to—

The phone.

"Hello," he said cautiously.

"Is that you, Martin?"

Although the voice wasn't all that familiar, he knew who it was.

"Oh, hello!" he said, digging for the enthusiasm. "I was going to call you."

"Of course you were," Richard's mother said. "But thank goodness your mother found the time. So it's true? They're off somewhere? He's gone from work?"

"Yes. He's taken indefinite leave. Compassionate leave, is what they said. He left Dunkers Green as the contact number."

"You've called the time-share?"

"Yes."

"Did you ring the ashram in Bridgetown?"

"Of course."

"How odd," she said. She was almost eighty, hard to ruffle. "And yet not terribly, when one thinks about it. It's going on four days, isn't it?"

"Exactly," he said.

"I think we need to give them a week or two before we demonstrate our concern," she said.

"Yes," Martin said.

"But you're concerned, aren't you? You're one of the closest to them; I know that."

"You yourself said it was odd," he said.

"I did. One moment please." He heard her cover the mouthpiece, the rich murmur of her voice when words were indistinguishable. "I think we'd like to come down there. Justin and I. Would that be all right?"

"Absolutely," Martin said.

"Good then, it's settled. We have a key. It's a delicate situation, isn't it?"

"That's right," he said.

"Good-bye, then."

"Good-bye."

"He tried to turn their daughter against her," Ruben whispered stagily as he stood yet again in the open doorway. He seemed, these days, almost always to be standing there, a fixture or a ghost. If only she could believe in ghosts. "But Cindy told Jenny everything. I say good for her."

"Ruben," she said wearily, "I've got class in five minutes. Why are you telling me this?"

"I don't know. Entertainment. Gossip. I thought you'd want to know."

"I don't want to know anything," Lauren said.

"Julia's in rehab again."

"You told me."

"I was lying. This time she's really in. I dropped her off this morning."

"Oh."

"You think I'm being a drama king? I'm just giving you the facts. Maybe that way, when we begin the slow lynching of your absent husband, you'll have something to fight with."

"That's not—" She stopped herself and stared at his wizened face, his straggly beard. It was hard to believe he and Lazlo were the same age. It was hard to believe they'd been friends for thirty years. "Whatever," she said. "I've got to run."

"Am I harassing you?" Ruben said, as she gathered her things and pushed herself and him out of the office.

"Not yet," she said.

"Well," Richard's mother was saying as she smoothed the lap of her dress for what must have been the tenth time, "I do think it would be a bit intrusive to be poking about at his work."

"I agree," Martin said.

"It's all terribly tricky," Richard's father said, his voice husky from exhaustion and age. "I'm not sure what it is we're about here. I'm not even sure why we are here."

"Well, it isn't an emergency," Richard's mother said.

"Of course not," Martin said.

They all sat in the living room with their shoes lined neatly in the hall, as the owners preferred it. They must have been sitting there for ten minutes, but was it really only that long?

"Richard is a good boy," Richard's mother said.

"An excellent young man," Richard's father said.

"I'm afraid it's a little unnerving, is all. I mean, the notion that you can stop the world and get off," she smiled, repeating what Martin had conjectured, "it does seem to be like them. They're adventurous. They *want* to live. I admire them both tremendously."

"I do, too," Martin said. What was it about talking to old English people that turned him into such a smarm?

"When do you think you'll go home?"

"I don't know." He looked at his socks—he'd been wearing the same crusty pair the last few days. He hoped no one could smell them. Maybe they didn't smell.

"And your wife is . . ."

"Hanging in there," he said.

"I believe your mother might come over if she finds something to do with your father."

Martin laughed. "That's always the trick."

"Is he . . . progressing?"

"He's hanging in there."

"You Americans like to hang in there," Richard's father said.

"Justin!"

They laughed. She stood, smoothing her dress as if she were wearing an apron. "I suppose I could make some tea. Or perhaps something stronger?"

"Stronger," Justin said.

In the kitchen, as Martin poured a drink for Justin, who'd been unwilling to come in from the warmth of the living room, Richard's mother readied tea.

"Lemon?" she said.

"Yes, please."

"Then you put it in there, like that," she said under her breath. "Just so. Yes."

And he strangled back a laugh.

"What is it?" She looked frightened.

"I think I'm a bit on edge," he said.

"Of course. Of course."

They went together into the living room, carrying tea and scotch. Richard's father was dozing in the big leather chair.

"Drink?" she said softly.

"Hmm?" He opened his eyes. "Well, maybe not. Martin, would you do the honors?"

He'd thought he'd just have tea, for once. He looked at the amber single malt, the way he'd poured it to fill the glass just so. He sat across from them on the sofa, and set the scotch neutrally on the coffee table, like an ornament.

"I'll get you some tea." Richard's mother went off back into the kitchen.

Martin waited. Justin looked at him, smiling.

"This is some pickle," he said. "You'd call this a pickle, wouldn't you?"

"It's been a pickle for a long time," Martin said.

"Eighteen months," Justin said.

Martin was surprised by the exactness with which he knew it.

"We love your sister very much," Justin said.

"I know," Martin said quietly.

"They are a wonderful couple."

"Yes."

"So." Richard's mother returned with a fresh cup of tea. "Where were we?"

"Here," Justin said.

"I think what I'll do," Richard's mother said, "is call Emma and let her know where things stand."

"I was going to call her," Martin said.

"Of course you were. But it's better, isn't it, coming from her mother?"

Martin picked up the scotch and sipped it. It was the thirty-year-old that Elizabeth had let him open after Richard had vanished. It was incredibly smooth, and then as sharp as an ice pick. He sipped it again.

"Good, is it?" Justin said.

Martin nodded in midswallow.

"They have such a lovely home," Richard's mother said. "I'm sure they'll come back."

"Quite sure," Justin said. He raked his thick moustache with an index finger. "Quite so."

Hmm, Martin thought he heard himself say. He took another sip of the scotch and waited for it to occupy his head.

When evening came they sat at the table in the kitchen and ate buttered bread and presliced meats rimmed with jelled fat and little pickles and some very mayonnaisy potato salad. Justin and Paula drank cold water. Martin worked slowly on the scotch. Their baggage—they'd flown in from Ireland, where they had retired to—hadn't moved from the front hall, as if they were awaiting an invitation. He wanted to say something gracious. On the flight up to see them not long after her diagnosis, Elizabeth had later admitted to him, all she wanted, all she *really* wanted, was for the plane to crash. *Then they just sat around all weekend and stared at me,*

she'd said. *Like they were waiting for me to die right there.*
Later she decided that they were sweet and attentive. It
was hard to figure them out. Anything could be true
about them.

"I'm sleeping in the study," he blurted out.

"Oh good," Paula said. "Then we'll take the guest
room."

While she and Justin saw to the dishes, he cleared
himself out of the guest room and made the bed to look
new. There was a room next to the guest room with an
exercise mat and a futon mattress on the floor, but he
certainly didn't want to be that close. He brought his bag
down to the study. He was feeling better. Maybe it was
true what they said about really excellent single malt—
maybe he wouldn't get a hangover.

He took their bags up all in the same trip—heavy,
boxy buggers from the midsixties, he guessed. The lug-
gage felt like it held weeks' worth of clothing. He knew
they didn't like to be uprooted. They liked everything just
so, but they wouldn't complain.

"So you're all set," he told them as they dried dishes in
the kitchen.

"Thank you so much, Martin," Paula said.

"Cheers," Justin said.

"Good night," he said.

"Good night," they said.

He lay on the built-in bed in the study, beside the
shelves of books about getting pregnant and getting
even. He never slept well without Lauren next to him
and the kids near. He'd either turn in relatively sober and

wake intermittently and for prolonged periods, or he'd try it blasted out of his mind and have one bolt of sleep and be up for two hours trying to cut up the hangover and then sleep for a last hour. He was now more into the latter sequence, even though he felt quite helplessly clear, that sense of distance between him and Lauren and the kids beginning to overwhelm him, as if he'd have to swim the ocean himself just to get back to them. What was it that he was always trying to escape?

As if there was a single answer—a force that could push him into another way of life. It was more complicated than that, more typical. Sometimes he felt a serenity, or not exactly that, but the possibility of it. But what or where was it? Was it death? Was it Lauren? Was it the children? Was it the past? Over the last eighteen months, at odd moments he'd be looking at a particular spot—the empty, wind-sheltered deck at the top of a battlefield observation tower, a patch of green grass on a remote soccer field, a pristine, hilly apple orchard right as the trees bloomed white in spring or flamed out in fall—and it hit him that he was looking for a suitable place to die. A place of isolation and comfort. A place on both a grand and a small scale, where the infinitesimal quality of his own life relative to all others could be enveloped in something not unlike a womb.

Where *was* she?

Nothing Sparks told him was news. He knew about the three new spots on the liver, the growing lesions on the spine and sacrum. He knew they wanted to zap her ovaries and she wouldn't let them. There wasn't a thing he didn't know.

"It's sad, really," Sparks said, not smiling, combing a loose strand of gray-blond hair out of her eyes. "We can offer her comfort. We can offer her quality of life. But she feels we're falling short, because we can't offer her a cure. Do you know what she told me last week? That she wasn't going to be one of those young women who die on Taxol. Sometimes I think she thinks that because we can't cure her, we're just trying to kill her. That we just want her out of the way."

Martin nodded, unwilling to contradict her.

"Of course, I'm not surprised she's left. She'll come back, though. She has to."

He shook his head. "My mother always thought she'd have to come back to the States. She's very strong. She doesn't have to come back to anywhere."

"Well." She checked her watch. "I don't know about that. I'm afraid I have another appointment."

"I'm grateful for your time."

"It's always hardest on the family," she said.

On his way to the tube, he tried to remember what he'd liked about Sparks from their other meetings. That she spoke directly to Elizabeth and never to him. That she was older than he'd expected. That she had a slyly frontal and yet reassuring delivery of the news. The disease was *easing out of control,* but she could *live with very little liver.* Lines like these, when he recalled them, made him laugh out loud. But when he first heard them, he was just writing them down to share with everyone else and even with Elizabeth, who tried so hard to listen that sometimes she couldn't remember anything. He'd read back his notes like a transcriptionist, and in Sparks's syntax they could find both the facts and even some comfort, if not exactly hope. From Sparks's view there had never been any hope. She hadn't been supposed to make it to New Year's. Now New Year's was in the rearview mirror, just another date. She was still alive. What did Sparks know?

But he'd felt his sister's humiliation. She didn't want to return to Baltimore because it would be a form of surrender. She didn't want to give up her breasts or her ovaries. And how sick she must have been of everyone's second-guessing—she hadn't pursued the right career, married the right man, chosen the right treatment, lived the right life. Their mother had once told her that if she died, it would be her own fault. Their mother was kind of like Vince Lombardi, and she easily forgot the harsh, exhortative things she said. It was important to find blame in someone else's dying because that meant it couldn't happen to you. But someday, he knew, he'd wake to find a lump or rise from the toilet to the evidence of a blood-black stool or feel a strike in his brain or at his heart that would be the last thing he ever felt. Everybody got a turn. There should be no sense of humiliation about it.

As he stuck his key in the door of Elizabeth and Richard's home, it opened and there stood his mother.

"Hello," she said evenly.

"Hey," he said. He wrapped his arms around her and

kissed her. Every time he saw her she seemed leaner and more muscular.

"You still love your old mother?" she said.

"Of course!"

He moved past her to hang up his coat, and there was his father, standing like something being propped up from behind, his belly lapping over his waist, his face puffy and yet drawn.

"Dad!" Martin said.

"Hey there."

They hugged. It was impossible not to love hugging his father, who was sweet and warm and soft. When Martin felt him begin to sob, he pushed gently from him and finished hanging up his coat on the tree. The tree was nearly full now. There were a lot of people in the house. He didn't feel oppressed by it.

"So?" he said, turning to them. "I can't believe you came."

"Of course we came," Martin's mother said. "Why wouldn't we come?"

"Your mother insisted," his father said.

"You insisted, too," his mother said.

"It's great you're here," Martin said.

Then the air seemed to go out of everything, and he was stuck with the fact that they were there and there were two more old people in the kitchen.

"What happened to your hand?" his mother said.

"Nothing. I had to break in to get in." He was gratefully surprised that Lauren hadn't told them.

"We had a key," his mother said.

"So did we," Paula called from the kitchen.

He shook his head and kept his mouth shut.

"So what did the doctor say?" his mother asked.

"Not much." He walked into the kitchen and they followed. Now they were all in the seventy-thousand-dollar kitchen. That's what he thought every time he saw it. Seventy thousand dollars. "She said she was sure they'd come back."

"Of course," Paula said. "I think they're having kind of a holiday, really."

"I got out of Richard's boss that three months of that compassionate leave are with salary."

"Three months?" Martin's mother said.

"I thought we'd agreed we wouldn't trouble his work," Paula said.

"It was just a chat," Martin said.

"A chat?" Justin laughed. "Calling his chief to have a chat? I don't think so."

"I hope you didn't make them too concerned," Paula said.

"I didn't," Martin lied.

"Anything else?" his mother said.

He poured himself a glass of water from the sink while they looked at him. "No."

"I think we could all go on back home then," Paula said quietly.

"Right," Justin said.

"Sitting in their house and waiting for them like this is wrong," Martin's mother said.

"Exactly," Paula said.

"You've done what you could," his father said.

"Right," Justin said.

They were all still looking at him, they hadn't stopped looking at him.

What the hell *was* he doing here? He'd even failed to ask Sparks the one question that he should have. Did she have three months? Elizabeth never asked that kind of question; it was a betrayal for him to. Though Sparks had left any mode of inquiry open: *It's hardest on the family.*

"Does she have three months?" he asked them.

"Martin!" Paula said.

"As long as she's alive," his mother said, "I have hope. That's what I believe."

"Me, too," his father said.

"Absolutely," Paula said.

"Right," Justin said. It was all he seemed to be saying lately, but he *was* eighty.

"I don't know if what they're doing is wrong," Martin said, looking at each of them. "But it doesn't feel right."

"*You* don't feel it's right." Paula seemed to be talking to a dish towel she was folding. "That's a judgment you're making, dear."

"I don't know what to feel," he said.

"There is hope," his mother said. "I have hope."

"That's not enough," he said.

"Why?" Paula asked, still folding the small dish towel. "Is there something else? Something, perhaps, that you think we're missing? Do tell us, dear."

At dinner, at a shabby Indian restaurant near the tube station, he drank beer steadily and barely spoke. The chicken vindaloo was all thigh meat, and the peas were gray, and the potatoes so soft they collapsed into a puddle whenever he tried to fork them. What *were* they talking about? It was the weather or a vacation one pair of them was thinking of taking or the expense of living in one city or another. It was what people had to talk about when they were just getting started after something tender, delicate, and unspeakable had passed among them. Before this whole awful year, in the previous whole awful year, he had once confessed to Elizabeth that he and Lauren divided their life into the before and after of her diagnosis. Oh, she'd said, I wish you wouldn't think of it that way. I don't think of it that way. It's a journey, it's not a division. But he hadn't gotten beyond that yet. He was thirty-eight, and he wanted to look at all of this squarely, and sometimes it made him feel like he was twelve and sometimes it made him feel like he was seventy, and perhaps he would never feel that he was getting it all the way he needed to get it to get through it.

"It's not terribly good, is it?" he heard Paula ask him through his wretched self-absorption, and he looked up to see her nodding at his plate.

"No," he said, "it isn't."

"That's all right," she said. "It'll get better."

The others laughed at this, an apparent joke, and he laughed, too, although he wasn't quite sure what it was he was supposed to be laughing at.

They split the check and began their way back slowly, as if trudging through snow, and he wondered if getting to be old and being old were like always having some kind of weather that you had to make it through, even when there was no weather at all. He walked at his father's elbow, and soon the others were far enough ahead so that he felt like it was just the two of them, his father panting at each step. He walked with a limp. The clouds seemed suddenly to be descending, and Martin worried they'd be caught in the rain.

"It'll hold off," his father said. "You can go on ahead, if you want."

"I don't mind being rained on."

"It won't rain," his father said. "I can smell it when it's going to rain, and I can't smell it, so it won't."

It began to rain.

"Shit," his father said.

They both laughed.

"It's only rain," Martin said. They didn't bother walking any faster; his father couldn't. The rain was falling more frequently. Soon they wouldn't be able to feel each individual drop, there'd be so many.

"I have the key," his father said.

"Maybe Paula or Justin took theirs."

"I don't think so. Could you run ahead?"

"They'll be all right."

"Okay."

It was a furious downpour, and he had nothing to cover his father with, and there was no shelter from it anywhere.

"Lots of big puddles!" his father shouted.

"I know!" he said.

"Do you think we should swim for it?"

When they arrived they were both soaked, and everyone else was standing dryly under the short roof over the front door.

"You have the key," Martin's mother said.

"I know," his father said. He wrestled it from his sopping pants pocket and with a trembling hand gave it to her.

"Hot baths for you two," Paula said as they dripped into the front hall.

"You've got him?" Martin asked his mother.

"Of course." She was already mopping his father's head dry, and then she kissed him softly on the lips. He seemed to be shaking all over. "You go on up."

On the steps Martin stood looking down at them. From the kitchen came the chime and clatter of Paula readying tea and Justin trying to help her. His mother kissed his father again while he shivered and couldn't seem to say anything. Martin went up the rest of the stairs and threw down a bath sheet.

"Leave us the shower," his mother called.

"Okay," he said.

He waited to see if his father was going to drop in the front hall, and when it was apparent he wouldn't, Martin shut himself into the bathroom with the tub and stripped off his clothes while the water ran and slowly turned warm. Then he got in and slowly, slowly sank down until he couldn't hear anything.

"That is one sorry door." The guy from Potterstown Overhead peered at it while keeping some distance. "You're lucky that thing didn't fall on your head."

"Can you fix it?"

He shook his head. "If it hadn't of fallen, I could. You

can jerry-rig practically anything for a while. But a big old wooden door like that, cracked up like it is," he said, still shaking his head. "You put it in your fireplace. Insulated aluminum. Light as silk, and runs as smooth as it, too. Practically will keep the whole house warm. That's the way to go."

"You want me to get a whole new system?" Lauren said.

"They don't make doors like that anymore. Everything it's attached to is part of that door."

"Nuts," she said.

"No one wants to go spending fifteen hundred on a new system if they don't have to." He grinned at her. "You have to."

"I'll be inside." She gestured a hand to indicate that he go ahead with it.

Fifteen hundred dollars? She pulled the checkbook from its hiding place in the kitchen cabinet. They had it.

In a trance Max lolled in front of the television. He wouldn't even come out to meet the guy, and he usually loved men in hard hats. "That door's going to fall again," he'd said. "I don't want to be there." "It can't fall again," Sarah had said. "It's already fallen. It's *on the ground*." And then they'd started in on each other. Now she could hear Sarah still pouting from up in her room.

"You awake?" she asked Max.

"Yeah," he said, not turning from the television.

"We're getting a whole new door."

"Okay."

As she trudged up the stairs, Sarah launched into a keening moan. Lauren opened the door to her room a bit wider.

"You always take his side!" the girl cried between sobs. "He gets to watch TV, and I get sent to my room. It's not fair!"

"We're getting a brand-new garage door," Lauren said brightly.

"When's Daddy coming home? I want my daddy."

"Soon," she said hopefully.

"You don't know, do you? You don't know when he's coming. *Soon* means you don't know. That's what you always say when you don't know."

"Sarah—"

"Maybe he won't come home because he doesn't like you anymore."

Lauren gasped and then tried instantly to cover the hurt. "I am sure Daddy loves all of us," she said. "You can come talk to me when you calm down." She shut the door partly closed.

"I'm never going to calm down," Sarah shouted after her.

The phone rang. Lauren glared at it. Sarah popped from the room, wiping her face.

"Let it ring," Lauren said.

"No." She darted past her and plucked up the phone. "Daddy?" she said.

Lauren snatched the phone from her and set it back down. "I *told* you not to answer it."

"It was Daddy!" Sarah cried.

"He can call back," Lauren said. "Now go to your room."

"I hate you," her daughter said, quickly, as she closed herself behind the door. "And when I grow up, I'm gonna hate you more."

"That's nice," Lauren muttered under her breath as she scooped socks and shirts into the clothes hamper. "That is really nice." When she dialed Star 69, it came back as untraceable. She wiped down the sink in the kids' bathroom and sprayed an organic antimildew agent onto the shower curtain. Still the phone didn't ring.

"You awake?" she called down to Max.

"Yeah!"

She knocked lightly on Sarah's door.

"What!"

She ducked her head in. "Was it really Daddy?"

"I don't know," she admitted.

It was between five and six, the time the phone and credit card people usually called. That was probably who it was.

"Can I watch TV?" Sarah asked.

"All right."

Sarah got up and hurried downstairs. It was impossible to keep them to the hour limit when you had them on your own. It was impossible to keep the bathrooms clean, the recyclables in order, the newspapers stacked, without the television. She'd give them another half of a show, and then, she swore, that was *it*. She refolded the towels over their racks and pulled the blinds in both their rooms and set the night-lights on. Just a few more minutes, and then she could face them.

"Hello!" someone called from the kitchen. At first she started, thinking it was Martin. Then she remembered the door guy.

"I'll be right down," she called.

In the kitchen he stood reading the stuff on their refrigerator door. He was smiling. "Come on and see what I've done."

From the back of his truck the old garage door stuck out in dismantled panels. The garage ceiling had been stripped of its various mechanisms. A light wind rattled the leaves against stacks of toys and the clutter of bicycles. Big flakes of snow had begun to fall.

"No door," she said.

"No door. I'll bring it by tomorrow and install it."

"Okay," she said. The last time they'd left the door open all night the garbage had been ransacked by animals large enough to leave streaky tooth marks. At least the weather wasn't anywhere close to good, or the weirdos who were always there would be playing basketball in the dark.

He climbed into the truck and drove off with her door. When she looked again she realized her eyes were stinging. She seemed to be a little blinded. She felt her way inside and popped a migraine pill.

She prepared dinner and pried the children from the television and sat at the table with them and tried to eat and keep a place inside her head from which she could still see and figure out things. Then while Sarah did her homework, she bathed Max, and while she read him bedtime stories Sarah bathed herself, and the phone didn't ring and Max finally laid himself down and willed himself to sleep. She combed Sarah's hair out, her face resolute, and read to her and then let her read to herself while she organized her papers for the next day.

At last she was in her own room, sorry about the garage door and sorry that everyone had gone to bed unhappy. She had to do better. Tomorrow she'd make it to the store and buy treats and cook their favorite dinner. Tomorrow the migraine wouldn't be there. Tomorrow there would be a new door.

She slept, or thought she'd slept. When she woke, or when she became aware that she'd always been awake, her chest was tight with an inexplicable but loud pounding that muffled her ears. She put her hand to her chest and felt her heartbeat. She got up and went to the window, the pounding growing louder. Then she knew what it was and instantly she felt better, light. The weirdos were playing basketball in the snow.

EVENING

The line into the Fine Arts Program headed downstairs through the cafeteria and then up into the gymnasium, and Martin still hadn't figured out what was wrong with the camcorder. It was supposed to zoom in, but every time he got half the distance there, it dissolved into blurriness. After watching the afternoon performance, Lauren had given him Sarah's exact onstage position. But by the time he found a seat in the gym, he was stuck in the tenth row, too far out to get a decent shot of her.

Mrs. Stingle came out on the stage and offered various announcements, rules, and mild scoldings, as if the audience were all her students. Finally the three-piece orchestra of the special-ed teacher, the phys-ed teacher, and the music teacher struck up, supported by a recent graduate on the violin, and the first of the acts marched out. The kindergartners and the special-ed class sang a song about purple—the theme, this year, was colors—then a section of first grade gave a spirited rendition of golden, and Martin played and played with the camcorder and still could not get it to bridge the distance. A tie-dyed ensemble offered a multicolor song, and then the light darkened and his program informed him that this was it, and he wheeled around and focused his camera on the rear of the packed room and out came Sarah's second-grade section, in white top hats, white T-shirts, and blue skirts or pants, waving American flags. They sang, he was certain, the same song he had sung in an elementary-school play thirty years before, while marching like soldiers with their flags held like rifles to their shoulders. Up onstage they came, almost briskly, and one group retreated to the wooden bleachers while four kids manned one microphone stage left, and Sarah and another girl commanded the microphone stage right. In Sarah he could clearly see, when he finally solved the blur of the zoom lens, a little of the ham and a little of the wannabe. She looked stunning. Her wavy, knotty hair was combed out in wild tresses, and her pale face was ablaze with a smiling glee. The piece she recited she'd written herself, and it was about how red must be the most important color of all, because people always said red-white-and-blue, not blue-white-and-red, and it was the second-longest recitation of the entire section, and she offered it without a single hitch, at almost exactly the right speed, and he was proud.

Afterward he shut off his camcorder and waited for the show to be over. He had a coveted aisle seat, but beside him the Italian guy from around the corner who ran a bicycle shop and had about thirty grand worth of toys in his backyard (*numbers or drugs,* the neighbors whispered, as he rode his John Deere industrial tractor-mower around his half acre or his daughter blared the latest Britney Spears from the Bose CD stereo system in her wired playhouse, *he's Sicilian*) kept doing the European thing and invading his body space. The curtain closed for another set shift, and out strode a plain-looking third-grade girl to stand at the microphone by herself. Martin felt his heart pinch for her, though she didn't look terrified. She just looked uncertain. She nodded at the music teacher and the music teacher nodded at her, and distinctly he heard the first strains of "Somewhere Over the Rainbow." She sang in a thin, steady, unremarkable voice, its subtle underdevelopment offering sketchy variance between high and low notes, the differing pitches caught more by volume than tone. All by herself, in front of the shut curtain, in the stuffy gym, she sang, her hands clenched to her sides in fists, her feet never moving, still except for the lilt and sway of her compact upper body. By the middle of it, he felt his eyes welling, and he knew the Italian was watching him, and just as he reached to dab the tears before they escaped, the Italian turned to face him, taking him in, then turned back, crossed his arms over his belly, and shook his head.

In the hall outside their daughters' classroom, the Italian's wife murmured to him, "Sarah had the big lines, eh?"

"Everyone did well," he said, not wanting to engage her limited English, knowing that she was so unhappy here she slept most days, as if waiting out a permanent hangover.

"Yes," she said. "Sophia, she had no lines."

"Next year," he said.

The husband would not look at him.

Sarah came out and he took her hand, and they bumped down the hall filled with familiar strangers.

"I'm proud of you," he told her, when they were outside.

"The teacher said I talked too fast. Did I talk too fast, Daddy?"

"No."

"Why did you have that camera pointed at me the whole time?"

"I'm making a video for Aunt Elizabeth," he said. "She asked me to."

"Today?"

"What?"

"I mean did she ask you today?"

"No," he said, as they crossed the street, passing parents in clusters talking in quiet, apparently cheerful conversation as their kids tugged at them. "A while ago."

"Hey, Martin," a woman from around the block called to him. "Nice to see you back." Her mother had died a few months ago. "How is she?"

"Hanging in there," was all he could say.

She squeezed his forearm. "That's good. You're a good brother."

They crossed the street and cut up their path and into the house. Lauren sat at the kitchen table, reading the newspaper.

"How was it?" she asked.

"It was great," he said. "Sarah was great!"

"Jenn fumbled a line," Sarah said.

"Don't gloat," he said. "Any messages?"

"Just the dean."

He picked up the portable and took it into the study. The dean answered on the first ring. Martin spoke, the dean spoke. It was all quite cordial. He had an interview at nine A.M.

"I know you must be jet-lagged," the dean said. "But we need to do this. For the family's sake and for our sake."

"I understand," he said.

"I'll see you then."

"Thank you."

Now he felt fuzzy headed. He hadn't felt that way watching the show, watching that girl sing. He'd felt incredibly sharp, clear, alive, in a tenuous way, just like her voice had seemed. Now he was numb. An interview. He dropped the portable on the foldout futon and switched on the computer. He began typing. What Jane Wilson was like the first day of class, what he remembered from all the other days, exchanges they'd had. He knew he was caustic and sarcastic in class. He knew that he'd said any number of complicated and culpable things. He knew he hadn't called Psychiatric Services about her. She had four other teachers. It wasn't only about him.

He felt a hand on his shoulder and jerked around.

"I thought you were still on the phone," Lauren said.

"Kiss good night?" Sarah said.

"Oh." He kissed her good night. "Congratulations, sweetie."

"Thank you, Daddy."

She went off up to bed.

"I've got an interview at nine," he said.

"Lovely," Lauren said. She looked on the screen at his notes. "These look good."

"Uh-huh."

"They can't pin a suicide on anybody."

"You never know," he said.

It was never accusatory was how he would characterize it later, when he had time. It was investigative. They were trying to learn. They were trying to know. They had no opinion. They had no agenda—except for the truth. The provost, the dean of residential affairs, and the director of security sat around a table, and Martin in a sense sat with them. They weren't against him. They just wanted to know. His class was the smallest she had been in, and so perhaps he could shed even more light than the other professors. Nothing was tape-recorded. They took notes. He offered what he had typed the night before, and they politely declined.

"No one's on trial," the dean said.

"This has no effect whatsoever on your tenure case," the provost said.

"Look," the director of security said. "She killed herself. Nobody else killed her. There's no need to even think defensive."

They asked about the last day he saw her. He described how she'd come into class looking slightly hollow, slightly pasty, not as put together as she usually looked. He told how she laid her head on her desk—the little arm desk that the students sat in—and how he asked her if anything was wrong and she shrugged. She was wearing sweatpants and a sweat shirt and ratty sneakers. Well, can you pick your head up? he asked. Okay, she said. And she kept her head up the rest of the class. It was odd because she was usually the class talker. At the end, as she filed with the others from the room, he asked her if she was all right. Just the flu, she said. Get better, he said. She'd smiled shyly when she handed in her paper.

"That was it?" the director of security said.

"Yes."

"Did you call her afterward to check up on her?"

"No," he said. "I don't usually—"

"Did you call or contact her advisor in any way?"

"No."

"Did you talk to or contact anybody about this?"

He shook his head.

"Well, then," the provost said. "Thank you."

"Is that it?" Martin said.

All of them nodded. They rose. The provost, a man who had shaken his hand at various formal occasions, reached out to him.

"Good job, Martin," he said. He had a weathered yet firm clasp. Powerful and odd. "In the future, when you see or notice anything unsettling, you can be more aggressive. We all can be more aggressive."

"Okay," Martin said.

"Don't be afraid to get to *know* your students," the

provost said. "That's really what Lincoln College is all about."

"I understand," Martin said.

"That's important," the provost said.

"Good-bye, Martin," the dean said.

"Good-bye."

When he returned to his office, the message light was flashing. He picked up the phone to retrieve whatever messages there were, but there was no dial tone.

"Hello," a voice said.

"Hello?" he said. It was one of those weird times when the phone hadn't rung because he'd picked it up right when it was about to.

"Is this Professor Kreutzel?" the woman said.

"Yes," he said uneasily.

"This is Mary Lou Wilson. Jane's mom."

"I know," he said, his voice going soft. "I'm very sorry."

"I'm just, you know, calling around. Tying up loose ends. That kind of thing." Her voice sounded as if it would erode at any moment.

"How can I help you?" he said.

"Could you send me any papers you might have of hers? Anything like that?"

"Of course," he said.

"Maybe if there were . . . I don't know how it really works there, Jane just said she always loved it . . . but if there are pictures you know of . . . of her, you know, participating in a class, that kind of thing, you could send them."

"No one took pictures in our class," he said gently, "but I can ask around."

"That would be great."

"What else?" he said. "How else can I help?"

"She talked about you," Jane's mother said. "She said you were passionate about anthropology."

That made them both laugh, it sounded so odd, like two words had been uttered that did not belong together.

"I *love* anthropology," he said.

There was a laugh in that, then nothing.

"I'm sure that the college will be talking with you soon," he said.

"That's what they say."

She didn't seem to want to get off the line.

"Well . . . ," he said.

"Was she a good student? Did you like her?"

"Oh yes," he said.

"She was really a terrific kid. A terrific person."

"Yes," he said again, although he didn't really know her, and he thought it unfair to pretend.

"Well, I guess I should let you go."

"Okay," he said.

"You know what?" Her voice picked up again. "You're the only person I've talked to at that place who didn't ask me *why*."

He was silent, hearing her anger.

"As if I know. As if anybody could know."

"Yes," he said.

"I like that about you," she said. Then she hung up.

Each day he tried and she tried, at least twice, to reach them. Early in the morning and late at night, sometimes in the middle of the night. He also called the neighbor every other day, the guy always unfailingly patient. "I'm just not seeing them," he said, "and, you know, I'm actually looking."

"I wonder if I should hire somebody," Martin told his wife.

On the Internet, for "locating" plus "missing persons," he found 76,324 hits. It was a whole industry.

He called an old family friend who worked at the FBI and told him everything.

"All right, Marty. I'll see what I can do," the guy said.

He called back late the same day.

"The last we have is London," he said. "I'm sorry. But we'll keep looking. Okay?"

"Thanks," Martin said. "Did you check credit cards?"

"Everything," the guy said. "It's not a big deal to be very thorough very quickly."

Once he asked his mother during a turgid phone call what she thought.

"You need to let them be," she said. "It's obviously what they want."

"Do you think it is?" he later asked Lauren.

She looked at him wearily. "The point is, they're gone. One day somebody will come back."

"Somebody?" he said.

"So she just bugged off, eh?" Ruben was in his familiar position in the office doorway. "That's understandable. I wouldn't mind bugging off myself."

"Where would you go?" Martin asked, trying to be polite.

"Africa? Or maybe the Carribean. I'd take Julia and we'd just bug off. I mean *really* bug off, so that nobody would ever know what had happened to us. Cool, don't you think?"

"It doesn't matter what I think."

"So you've learned that, too? You're no longer our cocky son of a bitch."

"That would be David."

Ruben shook his head. He was practically slurring his words, but he wasn't drunk. There was a rumor he'd be "stepping down" as co-chair at the end of the year. "You have to be young to be a son of a bitch, and David is not young. He's a bastard, he's an asshole. He's kind of a cocksucker, too, I guess. But that son of a bitch is not young."

Martin just nodded and half smiled.

"You know what you're good at, Marty? You're good at taking the focus off yourself. That's a skill there, Marty. You work with that and you'll be all right."

"Right," Martin said.

"So your sister isn't coming back. Makes you feel pretty awful, I bet. But, really, isn't this what everybody secretly wishes for—the dying person going off to die by herself so that nobody else has to deal with the pain and unpleasantness of it? Kind of like what some animals do. Why, in some cultures—"

Martin stood. "I've really got to get back to work."

"What about that girl's suicide, Marty? They clear you in that?"

"Charming," Martin said. "Now could you get the fuck out of my office."

"I'm sorry, Marty." Ruben was grinning halfheartedly, as if he were sorry. Maybe he was. "I guess I was just trying to see how many buttons you had to push. I like you. I really do."

"I don't care," Martin said. "I don't give a rat's ass who likes me."

"That's the spirit. That'll only help you." He slouched off up the hall.

Martin locked the door after him. The phone rang, and he turned on his computer and waited for it to boot up as the phone kept ringing and dwindled into voice mail. He'd been sending her unanswered e-mails since he'd returned—just in case she was somehow checking—chatty messages that made no mention of her escape, piling in cute details about the kids, trying to lure her into a response. Now all the fucking e-mails came up, from the dean, the provost, the director of security, the chair of the Faculty Review Committee. He opened the one from his mother. A report on how his father was progressing. The guy had been sick for twelve or thirteen years, and every time he made the tiniest step toward improvement she offered, *I think he's really turned the corner this time.* Quintuple bypass with an endoarterectomy. Congestive heart failure. Prostate cancer. Congestive heart failure again. How many fucking corners could he turn? His mother had long since concluded that he no longer respected his father, and she ranted at him about it, and he'd learned to keep his mouth shut. He hit the REPLY key, typed in "Great!" and hit SEND.

Don't get him wrong. He loved his father. Loved how

they'd walked shoulder to shoulder with the rain coming down. His father could slog through anything. His father, through a thirty- or forty-year bath in depression, had apparently inured himself to anything ultimate. They'd been forecasting his death for thirteen years. All he got was slower.

Martin typed in Elizabeth's address and for the subject line wrote *Max.* She alternated between which of the kids she favored, but she loved playing favorites. It was another entitlement she exercised, like commanding him here or there. He paged through the last days for anecdotes. They'd been to the SuperGiant several times, and around town, and whenever Max encountered a heavyset person he'd point and say, "That man is really fat" or "Look how fat that woman is." Finally Lauren had pulled him aside and told him it wasn't nice to call people fat, that it hurt their feelings. Then they'd walked to the pharmacy, and on a bench in front of the building sat an enormously fat woman, the fattest they'd seen lately by at least a hundred pounds, humongously fat, extraordinarily fat, just really fat. Max stood there staring at her, his mouth slowly opening. Lauren led him away. He was speechless. "Honey, what is it?" she asked. "That woman," Max said, groping for words, "she was really . . . beautiful."

That story Martin tried.

"Could you come here and look at this?"

It was his wife calling as he got groggily from bed, the

late April sun already cutting the room into swaths of light and dark. Sometimes he thought daylight saving was worse than jet lag. And sometimes he luxuriated in the earliness of it, the end of the day more and more distant, as if more seemed possible.

"What?" he said.

She was in Sarah's room trying to argue her into getting dressed for school.

"Up there," she said. "In the corner. There's a stain."

He walked to the corner of the room, where the low bookshelves met the desk. On the ceiling spread a rust-colored pattern, a circle.

"The roof is leaking?" he said.

"The roof is leaking," she said.

He looked at it closer, a faint, large swirl with wisps of dark streaks. The roof was leaking. How much would this cost? He hurried toward Max's room. He was at the play table canoodling with a set of construction toys. Martin patted him on the head and headed for the matching corner. A fainter circle had entrenched itself. Matching circles opposite each other across the chimney. He pulled down the attic stairs and creaked up them. The attic told him nothing. In his own bedroom he put on slippers.

"I'm just going outside for a minute."

"Okay." Lauren sounded exasperated, but she'd give him this last minute.

Outside, he looked up at the chimney and at the roof near where the stains were. The wood under the gutter by Sarah's room had a four-foot crack down the middle, and by Max's room it was growing ragged where it met the chimney. He went back inside.

"You gotta come see this!" he called upstairs.

"Not now!" she yelled.

He went upstairs and took over Sarah, and Lauren pulled on clothes and went out. By the time she came back in, Sarah was almost dressed.

"The wood is rotting under the gutters," she said.

"Oh," he said.

"At least it's not the roof itself."

"Fuck this house," he said.

"Martin!"

He looked at Sarah. "Sorry."

"Daddy's mad," Sarah said, dragging the last word into three syllables, trying to be cute.

"No kidding," he said.

They hustled her across the street to school and then he looked up roofers while Lauren distracted Max. He reached only answering machines and one woman who promised that she'd pass along word to the field estimator. He was confident he'd hear from no one. *Easy*, he told himself, *easy*. He set down the phone, took Max from Lauren, and glanced at the calendar. They'd been gone seven weeks. He wondered again where the fuck they could be. Sometimes he concluded India, and sometimes he thought Amsterdam, and sometimes he imagined a tropical island. He wondered a hundred times a day what it was like to be cut off from everything you knew and always realized that that had happened to her, in one form or another, from the instant of diagnosis.

"See you," Lauren said, kissing him.

"Bye," Max said to her.

"Bye," Martin said.

From the window they watched her walk up the street toward campus.

"What do you want to do?" he asked his son.

"What do you want to do?" Max asked back.

Frankly, he wanted a shot of vodka. He poured himself a glass of water and slugged it down. "Whatever you want to do," he said.

"Wolf Hollow?" Max searched.

"That's fine."

He packed a picnic of peanut-butter foldovers, peeled sliced apple, orange juice, and wheat crackers. He tried to love these solo days with Max, and for the most part—after the fact—he did. But in the middle of it, he couldn't help feeling that there was something else he should be doing—housework or job work or something about Elizabeth—and he was distracted and easily annoyed. You had to give in to such days, had to give up doing anything you thought you wanted to do, and convince yourself that what you wanted most was to give in to your kid. A very basic concept, he knew, but he still had a hard time doing it.

When he turned onto the battlefield road toward Wolf Hollow, Max began to shriek at him.

"What is it?" he said. "What is it?"

"I want the forest," Max screamed.

"What forest?"

"The Wolf Hollow forest!" He kicked at the seat.

As far as he knew the Wolf Hollow battlefield was all large boulders that Max loved climbing on. There were no trees that he could remember.

"The forest," Max screamed.

"Okay, okay."

He drove around toward Wolf Hollow. A few parking spaces at the head of a thick grove of trees slipped by over his shoulder.

"There!" Max bawled.

"Where?"

"There." Max was crying. "The Wolf Hollow forest."

There was no one behind him, and he backed up and parked. It looked to be a wide, sloping field of trees, underbrush, and poison ivy, at the very bottom of which must be Wolf Hollow. A worn path cut through all the growth.

Max wiped his face with his hand and started ahead.

"Come on, Daddy," he said.

They walked hand in hand into the thick of it, where they couldn't see any roads or hear any cars. Everything was green and limby and leafy and smelled of spring. Clots of gnats bobbed and whirred.

"I have to pee and poop," Max said.

"I didn't bring any toilet paper."

"Then I just have to pee."

"You can do it here."

"Right here?"

"Yup."

"I've never peed outside before."

"It's easy," Martin said. "Here." He aimed the boy off

the path and pulled down his pants and underwear. "Now pee."

Max peed. "Wow," he said. "That was great." He looked down at his pants and pointed. "Oh no," he cried. There were a few drops of urine on the front of his pants.

"It's all right," Martin said, as he buckled him into his pants again. "It'll dry easily."

"Wow," Max said again. "This is a good place."

They hiked slowly down the path. At Wolf Hollow they crawled on and around and between the boulders and watched a television news team from the State Capital film a segment on how there was no place to bury all the bodies once the shooting was over. They kept having to refilm to get the right backdrop, and Martin had to keep maneuvering Max out of any shot. He felt his patience draining.

"McDonald's?" he offered.

"Yep," Max said, as if, despite the packed lunch, he'd expected it all along.

They walked up the slow path through the forest.

"Should I pee again?"

"If you have to."

"I don't have to," he said glumly.

"Another time?" Martin said gently.

The boy kicked at the dirt. "Okay."

They drove home with a Happy Meal, and while Max ate and began a half hour of television, he tried Elizabeth and Richard without success and then he tried the neighbor.

"It's Martin," he said.

"Of course it is," the guy said. "I can tell by your voice. Did you know that your brother-in-law's back?"

"What?"

"I saw him last night. He's definitely back. This morning, too. He's puttering about."

"I tried to call him."

"Maybe he's not answering his phone."

"Oh." He hesitated. "And my sister?"

"Haven't seen her, mate."

"Well," he said. "Could you do me a favor? When you see Richard next would you mind telling him to call me?"

"No problem, Martin. No problem at all."

"Thanks."

"Cheers yourself, mate."

He dialed Richard again. Still only the answering machine. "Richard, it's Martin. I *know* you're home. The neighbor told me. Would you call me, please? I hope you're well."

He stood by the phone while the television washed over Max in the living room. Come on, he thought. Call back.

"It's over," Max shouted from his chair.

"Could you turn it off, please?"

"It was a great show." He clicked off the television and came into the kitchen. "What now?" he asked.

"Healthy lunch?"

The boy sat in his chair, and Martin unpacked for him the picnic lunch. It wasn't yet noon. Max ate and began to look sleepy.

"I need to rest," he said.

"I'll read to you."

They sat on the sofa, and Martin read him a book about a mother bunny who got chosen to be the last Easter Bunny because she was so kind and good and fast at being a mother, and just when her strength failed on the last round of Easter basket delivery the grand old Father Easter Bunny gifted her with a pair of golden boots and she became faster and kinder and better than she could have ever imagined. It was another goddamn story that hit him, and he had to hide himself from Max as he brushed at his face.

"What's the matter?" Max asked.

"I'm sleepy."

"Me, too."

They leaned into each other on the sofa, and he felt himself dozing off. Then the phone rang and Max leaped up to get it, and he had to race after Max and Max beat him to the phone and was already talking into it, and "GIVE IT TO ME," he screamed at Max, and yanked the phone from his hand, and Max bawled and he could barely hear the voice on the other end—

"—is going on over there?"

It was Lauren.

"Oh," he shouted over Max. "I thought you were still teaching."

"Nope," she said. "Just checking in."

"Richard is back," he shouted as he pushed the crying child into the living room and switched on the television and the boy quieted himself. "Richard is back," he said. "I talked to the neighbor."

"But you haven't talked to Richard?"

"No."

"He's sure it's him."

"Oh yes."

"Well," she said.

The Call-Waiting line beeped.

"Gotta go," he said. He double-clicked the phone. "Hello?"

"Is this a bad time?" It was his mother. "You sound out of breath."

"Richard's back. I just talked to the neighbor."

"I told you they'd come back," she gloated. "They're even early."

"He didn't say anything about Elizabeth."

She ate something in his ear. "You know how she holes up after a long trip."

"They haven't returned any of my calls," he said.

"They will, they will. But this is good news. I wouldn't bother them too much, though. They'll get around to us. They're probably just exhausted."

"Whatever," he said.

"I'll leave a message, too. I wanted to tell you that your father is back in the hospital. Kidney failure. He's doing much better. But if I give you his number, will you call him? He's a little down."

"Of course," he said.

She gave him the phone number. "I'd better run."

"I love you," he said.

"You, too."

When he put down the phone he realized that despite

the television Max was crying again, and he'd been shouting to be heard. "Oh honey," he said. He picked him up and held him. The boy sobbed hard against him, his chest rigid, his heart pounding near Martin's. "I'm sorry," Martin said. "I'm sorry. I'm sorry. Can we call Grandpa?"

The next day at work, she handed in their grade sheets and listened with apparent interest to the news that not only was Annka taking over as the sole chair of the department but that David Lazlo would be returning from his sabbatical with the woman from Kansas and her two boys. She tried to summon disgust or revulsion but she only felt *so what*. And wasn't it remarkable that Cindy was moving forward with her hip replacement surgery despite having no one to lean on? someone asked her. She nodded but said nothing.

In the afternoon there was a knock at her door and there stood Ruben, his face sagging and his beard trimmed.

"You coming?" he said.

"Oh right," she said, pushing herself from the chair. She followed him down toward the quad.

"Where's Martin?" he murmured as they fell into the silence building around them.

"He's kind of on his way out of town," was all she murmured in return.

They stood with the others in a thick circle around a small patch of unpacked lawn beside which stood a bundled baby spruce tree. The president offered a brief invocation, the provost added a few words. Then two of Jane Wilson's sorority sisters lifted the baby spruce and set it in its hole.

"From the class of '03, for its dear friend Jane Wilson," the class president read from a small rectangular brass marker. "Your memory will grow in us all."

As the circle broke up, a workman came and began to drill the plaque into a small raised stone set in the ground.

"You know," Ruben said as he walked back with Lauren, "I'm not at all sorry I lost the co-chair."

"I can imagine," Lauren said.

She sat at the computer in her office, clicking through e-mail, trying to set aside whatever she felt about what awaited in London, about all those unknowable students out there, about their own uncertain careers. About life. Was it all really so uncertain? The dread would crush her if she let it. She was sick of all the migraines she let happen, sick of all the migraine medication she let herself take, sick of her optimism and naiveté and fragility and agitation. Life in the middle of all this? Life *was* the middle of all this.

Earlier than scheduled she parked at day care and stepped from the car. In the fenced yard she could see Max whipping around the plastic slide set with the other children, laughing and laughing, and she stood there for a moment before he saw her, before she let him see her, watching him.

"So," Richard said, sitting across from him at the kitchen table as they sipped tea and stared out the back French doors into the clipped yard, Martin's bag dropped in the hall, the place so still you could balance an egg anywhere in it.

"How have you been?" Martin asked.

"I can't complain."

"It's good of you to see me."

"Not a bother, really. I'm here. Now you're here. It's not like I had to do anything."

"Can I ask you what your plans are?"

"Of course. Of course. We're going to sell the house. I still have some time off left. There might be travel. Perhaps a posting to another city. Don't know, really. Beyond that, I mean."

"I see," Martin said. He wanted to be gentle, but he just didn't know. What was there to know?

"She, uh, she sent along some things to you." He reached into a stack of bags and boxes beside him on the table and pulled out a velour sack about the size of a fist. "Things she said she wouldn't be needing anymore."

"Thank you," Martin said, his face growing numb, as he tried to keep his features smooth, tried not to crumble, to let what he could happen.

Richard shoved the sack across the table to him. "It's what she wanted you to have. Most especially for Sarah."

"Should I open it?"

"If you like."

"I don't know what to do," Martin said miserably.

"Have some more tea," he said. He moved to the stove and brought the kettle over, poured it into the cups.

"*What* can you tell me?"

"What does it matter?" Again he sipped his tea. "What will it matter? That's all for each of us to sort out."

"Oh man." Martin got up and went to the doors. There was no longer any wood block for a pane, and he tried to see which pane he had broken, but now he couldn't tell. He'd never see her again. Maybe he had never seen her. Was that what this was all about? How for years—*years*—they'd never known each other. There'd been all that intensity, all that intimacy, as they'd grown up and fought their way out, broke all the rules and slammed around the house, their mother screaming after them. How Elizabeth promised that when she ran away she would take him. How he caught her packing without him and threatened to tell on her unless she stayed. But once out, once separated, along their own paths, was when the distance had begun. It was a failure of life, how hard it was to stick together, how impossible, and you had to find that other person, that lover, and then maybe there were kids, and for a time they were part of what you had, and then they would leave, and there would be only more distance between what you had known so well—what you had breathed every day—and what you would have now. Long-distance phone calls. Weekends. Maybe a week here or there. But not that seemingly endless, sealed-off world of when you were children or when your children were children, when you had each other all the time and it was both never enough and almost too much.

Now Richard was at the door with him. "I heard you broke down this thing," he said. "Mitch told me. He had some glazier in to repair it. I can see it, but only because I know."

"What a mess," Martin said.

He put his hand lightly on Martin's shoulder. "Maybe what I said is all a bunch of crap. But it's a bunch of crap I believe in. You want a beer?"

It wasn't yet ten o'clock. "Sure."

He brought two bottles to the table and opened them. "Glass?"

"No."

They drank from the brown bottles and looked out the doors and looked across the kitchen and looked at the table. And all he could think of was that one time they'd had to go for dinner, and she wasn't up to it but she'd gone anyway though she hoped it wouldn't be too long and it was; it was quite long. And how he'd sat there drinking with the rest of them, watching her endure it.

"So you're not going to open it?" Richard asked as he pointed at the pouch with his bottle.

"I'll open it with Sarah."

"That's nice."

Martin took a deep plunge into the beer, and when he came out he felt a bit more ready. "Did you give her some kind of ultimatum?" he said. "Is that what happened?"

Richard looked both perplexed and amused, maybe even a little hurt. "All along I've been doing what she told me to do. No more. No less. Just exactly what she wants."

"But why . . . why did she take herself away from us?"

He got up and went for two more beers, wanting only to

listen, trying to look casual about it. "Was it out of anger?"

"The choices she's making, they're very private," he said quietly, and Martin found himself latching on to his use of the present tense. "They go beyond the self, really." He accepted an opened bottle from Martin. "What she's trying to do is really quite beautiful."

"What if we wanted to find out more?"

"You Kreutzels." He shook his head sadly. "You don't know how to accept anything."

Martin looked at him carefully, the creases in his forehead deeper, more flecks of gray in the hair that hung over the tips of his ears. The pale hands were strangely calm. He thought they used to quiver slightly. It was getting harder and harder for him to see any difference between the way things had been and the way they were now. He could always sense the broad failure of how they'd all been with Elizabeth, but he was losing track of each specific one, his own pathetic, halfhearted, half-realized gestures, his self-involvement in his own guilt. But wasn't that better than looking away? Or was it just another way of looking past her? He'd missed too much, but it seemed so indeterminable.

"What if we wanted a funeral?" he said.

"Who said there needed to be a funeral?" Richard said sharply.

"I mean, just suppose."

"What's so great about a funeral? The dead don't know anything about funerals."

Hadn't this whole fucking struggle been between the

desperation to say the things you knew they wanted you to say (*Everything's going to be okay. You're doing everything right*) and to say the things you knew you shouldn't ever say, that they couldn't bear to hear (*You have to leave him. You have to come home*)? Or was it about what you did when there was nothing you could do?

"We don't need to be having these kinds of conversations," Richard said.

"But that's why I came," Martin said.

For a while he lay in the guest room, trying to sleep. That had always been the routine. They used to have drinks standing up in the kitchen, a little rest, then go out to meet Richard for lunch near his office. There was a Greek place on a walking street, and the one time he brought the kids they chased each other around a fountain. At meals Elizabeth would have hummus and olives and sip bottled water while he and Richard and Lauren, if she were there, would drink wine and dig into various types of flesh. He tried to visit every two or three months.

Back when she and Richard got married, eight or nine years ago, they asked Martin to drive them from the ceremony to the reception. Martha and his mother teased him about how he ought to wear a cap and uniform. Lauren sat beside him in the front seat of the rented white Cadillac, and they drove from the old downtown synagogue along the expressway toward Mount Washington. It was a misty, soggy day. Richard and Elizabeth sat very close in the backseat, sipping champagne, kissing, thanking him too profusely for driving, saying how they had really wanted to share this moment with them. Two new couples.

They pulled up a winding road to a hilltop glass house filled with catering people, a jazz band brought up from Washington, 150 celebrants. Martin opened the car door for his sister. She slid from the backseat all in white, the veil lifting over her hair like a petal. Later, as the band paused expectantly and the mist that clung to the windows seemed to have lightened against the falling darkness, Richard's sister raised her glass. "And do take care of our brother Richard," she said after whatever usual jokes she'd felt obligated to recite, and suddenly her voice was soft and tentative. "He is the only one we have, and we love him very much."

Now Martin descended the stairs and saw through the shut glass door of the study the back of Richard as he sat at the computer and Richard wheeled around and motioned him in.

"Jet-lagged?" he said.

"Yeah."

"I'm just finishing up here. And then we could go out for a bite to eat. How long did you think you'd stay?"

Martin shrugged.

"You can use the phone if you want."

"Thanks."

He sat in the kitchen, drinking water. The jet lag made everything seem even more unreal than it already was.

"Still in bad shape?" Richard called in.

Under the blue sky they took the Alfa Romeo with the top down, and he faced the wind and tried to feel it as fully as he could.

"Great weather," Richard shouted.

"Yes," he shouted back.

They went to the best Indian there was, a marble-and-leather place where the four of them had once gone together, a vast hierarchy of wait staff, a twenty-page wine list.

"I think I'll drop in at the ashram, so we haven't much time."

Martin nodded. They ordered immediately. He hadn't eaten in a day or two. When the beer came he took long sips and tried to feel more alert.

"What *do* you want to do?" he finally said. "We can't just let it dissolve into nothing."

"We can't?" Richard took his napkin and unfolded it in his lap. "Well, I can't worry about what you think is going on. There's too much that I have to do, and I need to be off again soon."

"I can feel it," Martin said, not touching the food. "I can feel the absence."

Richard looked at him. "You don't really believe that."

"I don't know what to believe."

"That's the problem. Everybody needs something to believe. That's exactly what I've been trying to tell you."

Martin ate silently, nothing he could right now taste. When they'd been here Elizabeth had been allowing herself a small nibble from everyone's dish, digressing from her rigid diet. *I'm being bad,* she'd said. She had a tiny sip from Lauren's wine. *Aren't I horrible?*

"Your mum called," Richard was saying. "She thinks she's coming tomorrow. To help out. To help with what? I said. It's what people do, she said. There's nothing to help with, I said."

"What about my father?"

"She didn't say. I think she was too stunned to be talking with me."

"I can understand that," Martin said.

The main dishes sat there, and Richard moved them farther from the center of the table.

"Look." He drew a pen from his shirt pocket. "Can I show you something from Epiphany that might help? The first thing they do with us."

Martin just looked at the food.

Richard turned the beer coaster over and drew a large circle. "This is all the knowledge there is in the universe." He drew a narrow wedge in the circle. "This is all the knowledge you know you know. Anthropological theory. How to try to raise your kids. You know."

"I know," Martin said.

He outlined a second wedge of the circle of about the same size. "And this is all the knowledge you know you *don't* know. Neurosurgery. Junk bond trading. Gardening."

"I get it," Martin said.

"And all this," Richard pointed to the rest of the area of the circle, beyond the two pie slices, "is all the knowledge you *don't* know you *don't* know."

"Oh." Martin sipped his beer and looked at the circle. "It's familiar, but it has a kind of optimism."

"See?"

"Yeah, I see."

"That's the beginning of everything," Richard said.

Martin began to peel the label on his beer.

"Would you take Epiphany?"

"I don't know," he said.

"If I told you I wanted you to take Epiphany, would you take it then?" Richard was leaning over the table now, with a rare enthusiasm.

"What would your asking me—" Martin cut himself off. For what seemed like the first time he felt himself understand that Richard had been with her all this time, that she hadn't been alone, that she'd had him, that he'd done that. "I just don't know," he said.

"That's good. I'll take that." He gestured to the waiter for the check.

"It's on me," Martin said.

"Do you want me to drop you anywhere?"

"No. You go on."

After he left, Martin went out to a pay phone. She answered on the first ring. It was quiet on the line between what he was able to relate, only a slight pinging echo from the satellites.

"I'm so sorry," Lauren said gently, when he was finished. "Why don't you just come home."

He traced the cool metal face of the phone. It wasn't so long ago and yet it was very long ago that he'd called her at the office once, on that Saturday afternoon when he was home with the kids while she was grading papers, and he'd just gotten off the line from London and he dialed her number, Max trying to jam one of the cats into the refrigerator, and he'd said, *When are you coming home?* in a voice that must have been terrible, because she'd said, *Why, what is it?* so desperately, so instantly frightened, and he'd tried to say something, anything, to express what he'd just heard, but all that came out was *Please come home,* each word like dust, and she'd said, *What, what,* and finally what was left to say, what he could say, what he cried into the phone was *Just come home.*

"Maybe she isn't," his mother said in that appallingly and yet soothingly matter-of-fact way of hers, as they sat outside his father's hospital room on his discharge day, waiting for him to finish a last session of physical therapy. "He never told you she was. I haven't heard you say that. And he didn't say that to me."

"Did you ask him?"

"Of course."

Martin stretched his legs, the unstitched leather flaps from his favorite old hiking boots dangling over the floor.

"You ought to be embarrassed," his mother kidded, pointing at the worn-out boots. "You're a grown man."

"Right," he said.

"Sometimes I've wondered . . . you know . . . whether I've been sensitive enough to the fact of her . . . you know."

"Her illness?" he said.

"Yes."

"Maybe," he said. "Maybe we've all worn each other out."

"Maybe." Her lips shut against each other, and she

shook her head. "You know the last thing she asked from me before she went away? She wanted me to go through all our slides and send her copies of some pictures of herself."

"Oh," Martin said. And his eyes blinked, and he could clearly see her lying in a bed somewhere surrounded by better images of herself, and how that could somehow help. And then too clearly it seemed to him he could see her at three—before he was even born—and at five when she'd first been allowed to hold him, and at fourteen, and at college, and on Wall Street, and at his and Lauren's wedding when Elizabeth and Richard had leaned toward the camera in the same leopard-patterned glasses frames when she didn't even wear glasses, and then . . . and then . . .

"There's a mother's right to know," his mother was saying. "And then the kids grow up. And who knows what the right is anymore." She sighed. "You'll find out."

"If I'm lucky," he managed to say.

"Don't be so morbid."

They sat there quietly, and finally he turned her wrist to look at her watch.

"You in a hurry?"

"I promised I'd be back for dinner," was all he said.

"Are you all right?" she said as she stroked the back fringe of what was left of his hair.

"No," he said. "No, I'm not."

"So what do you want?" Sarah eyed him warily as they sat on the bed in her room, the door shut. He'd awkwardly come in and held a finger to his lips as he closed the room off from Max.

"Aunt Elizabeth." He swallowed any emotion. "Aunt Elizabeth sent you something." From his pocket he pulled out the velour pouch and placed it in front of her.

"What is it?" Sarah said.

"I don't know. I didn't open it."

"You didn't?" She looked at him with disbelief.

"Nope."

"So you want me to open it and then call her, right?"

"You can't call her," he said. "You know I don't know where she is."

"So I'll write her a letter or something?"

"Something," he said.

She looked closely at the velour pouch and then looked back at the book she'd been reading. "Maybe I should wait until my birthday," she said.

"You can open it now," he said.

She tugged on the satin string and then grabbed hold of the bottom of the sack and overturned it. A pearl necklace and two gold earrings each with a dangling diamond dropped onto the bed.

"Wow!" she said.

"That's Aunt Elizabeth's pearl necklace," he heard himself say quite distantly. "And those earrings are what we all gave her when she turned forty."

"She's giving them back?" Sarah said. "I thought she liked them. And didn't Uncle Richard give her that necklace? What is she—dead?" She started to cry.

"Oh, honey." He reached for her and held her. "I can't say. I guess I think she is . . ." He shut his eyes and tried to see. "I guess I think she could be gone. Or maybe she's just sick of all this stuff. Or maybe she's . . . getting ready to go."

"Getting ready to die? People don't get ready to die." Sarah sniffled and wriggled from his grip. "We were supposed to go see her this summer. She wanted us to. I didn't want to. Won't I ever see her again?" She was weeping now. She picked up the necklace and ground it back into his hand. "I don't want this," she said. "Get out of my room. Get out now." She pushed the earrings and the sack from her bed. He again reached for her but she shied away.

"Sarah—"

"You *knew* what was in there," she cried.

"I didn't," he said, stopping to pick up everything from the floor. But of course he had guessed.

In the hall Lauren stood holding Max.

"I'm such an idiot," Martin said.

"I don't know." She joggled Max, who cooed and clung to her as if he were a baby again. "The whole thing is so impossible." She sighed and glanced at Max and looked back at him, her eyes still rimmed red. "I mean, whatever she's done is incredibly selfish," she said. "But it's also . . . it's also admirable somehow."

"I know," he said.

Then there was a knock from behind Sarah's door.

"It's your door," he said through it. "You can open it."

She poked her head out. Her eyes were watery, but her face was nearly composed. She held out her hand. "I changed my mind," she said. "I want everything. I want all of it, please."

He put his closed hand in her open one and opened it.

"What is it?" Max demanded.

"Girl stuff," Martin said.

Sarah quickly closed the door shut.

"What do I get?" Max said, tugging at Lauren's shirt.

Martin still had the deflated velour pouch and he held it up. "This?" he said.

"Oh." Max snatched it and wriggled his tiny hand inside. He pulled out something. "I found it," he said.

"I thought it was empty," Martin said to Lauren.

Max held out his hand.

"Oh shit," Martin said.

It was her wedding ring.

That night the college was spending fifty thousand dollars for a fireworks display for returning alumni. The students were long gone, and the fields were filled with people in their thirties, forties, fifties, sixties, who for one reason or another felt proud enough of their association with the place to shell out $250 each for the privilege of attending the weekend. The air was barely cool, it was early June, and Martin and Lauren sat holding hands on a spread underneath the darkening sky while the kids raced around intersecting with other hopped-up kids, shrieking and tickling while they waited.

"When's it going to start! When's it going to start!" Max demanded.

"Soon," Lauren promised. "Soon."

The twenty-fifth reunion class had a keg in a roped-off area, enveloped by thickening guys in bermuda shorts and button-down shirts and penny loafers, women with frosted hair and pastel blouses and plaid skirts. Martin used to think that the people who returned for such reunions were either preening their nouveau riche selves or—even worse—exhibiting the pathetic fact that college was the high point of their lives, but now he could see the comfort of it. A tourist train coming into the fake train station tooted its horn. There was a high whistle, and then the sky filled with bright pink streaks followed by a tremendous boom.

"Ow!" Max screamed. "Mommy! Mommy!" He ran to them and fell between their laps covering his ears.

He'd been waiting all day for this, and it only frightened him. On the lawn Sarah jumped up and down.

"Come on," she shouted at the sky. "Come on! More!"

Max kicked against the ground. "I want to go home," he moaned. "I want to go home."

Martin got up. "I'll take him."

"Let me," Lauren said. "You must be exhausted."

"What do I care about fireworks?" he said.

He picked up the whimpering boy and rested him against his shoulder. The sky boomed, and the boy curled tightly against him.

"Okay," he said. "Okay. We're going home."

He carried him out through all the families staring up at the sky, with one hand pressed to the boy's ear to muffle the next explosion. They passed close to the keg, and he felt how dry his mouth was in the slow onset of summer. They reached the street, and his sandals slapped against the empty sidewalk as explosion after explosion sounded behind him and the boy whimpered and sobbed.

"Almost there," Martin lied.

"I want to go home," Max sobbed. "Please, Daddy."

"We're going. We're going."

At the stoplight, more than halfway there, he turned for just a peek. Yellow fissures sliced the sky, shot through with bursts of blue and orange, and when the color dissolved as it fell he could hear the popping and whistling of more light to come. It was all artifice, he knew. He wanted to feel nothing.

Or he didn't know what he wanted to feel. When Lauren had come home that time from the office, and he'd managed to tell her what Elizabeth had told him, and they'd looked at each other and felt their life ripping away and changing at the same time, they stood in the front hall, the children retreated to the living room, and they held on to each other, while he buried his face in her shoulder and she soothed him, while she let him cry himself out. He cried, he felt, from the base of his skull, from his chest, from his lower back, from wherever the depths of where he could reach inside himself were, from wherever the grief was exploding inside him. When he was able to look again, the children came out cautiously to ask what was wrong with Daddy, and Lauren had to wipe her eyes for the moment and say, Nothing. He'd thought that was an end, the way he'd been able to let the grief tear into him. Maybe what he wanted was all that emotion to come back to him, so he could have it again and let it go. He knew he dreaded it, and he knew it might not be there, even if he sought it. Had he been going after it all this time, or had he been just avoiding it? Was it her intention to relieve him or deny him of emotion? Maybe he just wanted to feel it the way she intended it.

Now he saw their escape as some extreme extension of the simple fact that she had always refused to return, to come back to them. What a dreadful and complicated and bold thing she'd done, how, by depriving him and them of being with her, she had somehow probably saved something of herself. And it wasn't only that they could have been perceived as dogs on some shore waiting to devour her as soon as she drifted in on the raft of her illness—although certainly that was part of it. It seemed to him that in choosing to be among strangers and only with Richard, she had probably relieved herself of some of the essential humiliation that seemed to await them all on this passage, among the culture of the living. And, in some truer sense, she had never given in to her illness. And he could turn it around and around and see the two of them again—in the back of the white Cadillac he himself had driven, in the picture at his wedding to Lauren—and see how encased they had at some time been, encapsulated in their couple-ness. And that certainly was an answer. He could look at his children and know it to be true. He wanted to live. He could look at Lauren and know that there was so much more between them, unexplored, unknown, that he needed to reach, that he wanted to reach. He wanted her. He wanted the children.

"What is it, Daddy?" Max asked, his face tight against Martin's shoulder.

"Nothing," he said.

"Is it beautiful?"

"I don't know," he said, as they began to cross the street. But he kept glancing back at the sky. "Maybe you should look and see?"

She was gone, oh god she was gone. These had been years that death was everywhere, that he woke every morning and could not escape it, that he kept feeling he was missing everybody, that he had to keep living, that death descended, that it hadn't yet arrived. These were years that death was everywhere. He had never wanted them to end.